*Divertimenti*

# Divertimenti

SUNSTONE
PRESS

SANTA FE
NEW MEXICO

*The title calligraphy is by Shar Race,*
*and the typography and illuminated letters*
*are by Mina Yamashita at Sunstone Press.*

First edition

Printed in the United States of America

---

Library of Congress Cataloging in Publication Data

Adams, Robert Martin, 1915-
        Divertimenti / [Robert Adams]. -- 1st ed.
            p.  cm.
        "Written by Robert Adams for the pleasure of his friends"-
-Dedication page.
            ISBN 0-86534-222-9
            1. Epistolary fiction, American.  2. Historical fiction, American.
I. Title.
PS3551.D394D58    1994
813' .54--dc20                                              94-8526
                                                            CIP

---

Published by    Sunstone Press
                Post Office Box 2321
                Santa Fe, New Mexico 87504-2321 / USA
                (505) 988-4418 / *orders only* (800) 243-5644

*The Divertimenti*
*were written by*
*Robert Adams*
*for the pleasure*
*of his friends.*

◆

# CHUNDO AND THE AUROCHS

iterature in 5th-century France, or more properly Gaul, was by no means quiescent, though one has to admit that it flourished only here and there, only now and then, in small enclaves. A scattering of poets warbled in their separate isolations, none of them first rate, but a couple of them like Ausonius and Sidonius Apollinaris, civilized and inventive. In the mixture of prose and verse to which the age was attracted, the great achievement was Boethius' *Consolation of Philosophy*, but that was the work of a patrician, writing in the capitol city and consorting with the elite. Gaul could only admire from a distance the range of the author's erudition, the sustained coherence of his thought, the dignity of his vocabulary. Nobody ventured to imitate him. Throughout the empire language was a problem and not just for men of letters. Some inhabitants of Gaul and outlying provinces had lived within the empire as nominal Romans for five centuries and more, yet still spoke only a halting and very dialectical Latin. Some spoke hardly any Latin at all, posing problems not only for themselves but for their Romanized neighbors. Buying a horse or renting a wagon, one had to use the tongue understood by the owner, even if he called himself Munderic or Aregisel. In the daily business of life, linguistic compromises of a very low order gained frequent ascendancy, sometimes swallowing up an original Latin locution, or usurping its place entirely. In the market and on the road, makeshift language may have served the common man's turn well enough. But for writing an epic poem or an historical commentary, something more dignified and more widely comprehensible was required. From the viewpoint of a modern student, nothing can be imagined more interesting than an extended discourse in 5th-century argot. But the 5th century itself had no such perspective; writers were ashamed of their different makeshift languages because they barely resembled the classical dialects of Cicero and Tacitus. Though the classic authors could be read and perhaps appreciated, they could not be imitated. The minds and imaginations of 5th-century builders did not extend to the dimensions of their predecessors; instead, they built little chapels, often tearing down lofty temples to get materials for their own comparatively scrawny structures. In literature as well, cannibalization and resulting miniaturization were frequent. Thus without benefit of a critical commentator who might have defined contemporary practice and given it new shape or at least new direction, the last years of Roman Gaul glided almost silently away. For centuries the district had been protected by legions, by allies, by mountains and rivers, by fortifications, and above all by years of inward assimilation and accommodation. The barbarians who had settled in Gaul long ago were no longer rapacious looters; they had acquired some property of their own (not always gently), and were ready to defend it. They could not have been mere languid Sybarites, but they were not the marauding barbarians their sires had been. Thus a kind of ragtag patchwork tranquility prevailed in Gaul — not a formal peace but something more comfortable — a social peace floating on the warm waves of a general intellectual torpor. However agreeable, this potpourri of races, faiths, and ethnic groupings could organize little defense against the onslaught from the north which descended on Gaul starting about the year 400. Left to itself, Roman Gaul might have drifted quietly through a last season of social decay tempered by local disorder. Gaul as the Romans left it had no very exciting future. But in fact the district was not left to its own devices and as a social unit it had no future at all. For when the floodgates were thrown open (the year 400 is only approximate), authentic predatory barbarians in large numbers came pouring through. Some were in pursuit of comforts, amenities, and security somewhere further on; others were trying to escape from present dangers at their heels. They travelled as they had always travelled and preferred to live, in tribal units, sometimes as small as a single large family, sometimes in bigger but looser groups. They were hard to keep track of because their alliances were shifting and temporary. When four or five units banded together for a particular end, they were known sometimes by the name of one unit, sometimes by that of another. None of them could read or write, so their history of themselves was mostly legendary. They were proud of their ancestors, so that increased the number, though not the accuracy, of their traditions. They liked to maintain a distance from their neighbors, so they built few walled towns or urban complexes. Only rarely did one tribe mark off its territory from that of its neighbors; a river or a forest was about as much of a boundary line as they needed. They had access to few precious metals and set little store by them until contact with the civilized world corrupted them. They were famous for the simplicity of their domestic manners and the hardihood of their warriors.

Among these Germanic tribes, not very conspicuous or influential at first, appear traces of a people known as the Franks. As early as the third century they are perhaps mentioned in a marching song of the legions, and given less equivocal space on an early Roman road-map. Before long they are considerable enough to be divided into groups, of which the Salii are the most prominent. In 431 Salian Franks fought at the battle of Chalons (*the Catalunian fields*, as they were called) in which the Roman patrician Aetius, with the help of many allies, repelled Attila and his Huns. One of the early Frankish kings was Merovech, who gave his name to the dynasty of kings possibly descended from him. The son of Merovech may have been Childeric, whose son Clovis established himself in 483 as the ruler of almost all Gaul. The dynasty was known as that of the Merovingians.

Having entered the Roman empire as allies (*foederati*) of the slowly deteriorating central power, the Franks were not themselves centralized enough to take over all the civil authority in Gaul. Here and there they bargained with established possessors for a share in the arable land; but, the blackmail having once succeeded, they were likely to settle down and cultivate their new properties. They had, and continued to maintain, a monarchy with a headquarters at Tournai in modern Belgium. We need not suppose the court to have been very elaborate or ceremonious. There was not much in the way of a formal legal system, courts of law, systems of appeal, judges, attorneys, and so on — though there were codes of conduct, sometimes quite strict. But there were few codifications, recensions, or commentaries. The parliament, as we might be tempted to call it, was the king's counsel, a band of chosen warriors known most often as his "men" (*leutes*); when they were not fighting or looking for a fight, it was a point of honor that they be as idle as possible. They had little interest in display; the common costume might consist of breeches and tunic, with perhaps an animal pelt or pelts in winter. Armor and weapons accompanied the king's men a good deal of the time; they commonly carried a battle axe, a short knife, perhaps a lance. Approval of a measure brought before the counsel was signalled by clashing weapons together. A much-remarked feature of the Frankish court was that the kings, and those in the royal line, wore their hair very long — unshorn, in fact; to have one's hair cut, even under force or the threat of force, disqualified one from the succession. To pass the time, they did a lot of serious drinking.

Christianity had a long history in Gaul; but it impinged on the Franks only when their first king, Clovis, ordered them to convert. Knowing what was good for them, the Franks promptly converted — as promptly as Clovis himself had done when told to convert by his wife. Whatever the impulse behind the conversion of the Franks, who had always been instinctively and unquestioningly pagan, they believed as they were told without reluctance. They made no problems over the Arian subtleties into which they might have been inveigled, for example by the local Visigoths. In the matter of belief they were good soldiers, loyal subjects. Their doctrinal docility did not gratify everyone alike. Gregory of Tours, born into a Roman patrician family, educated by serried ecclesiastics, and granted episcopal authority at the age of 34, displayed a spectacular eagerness to vindicate his faith against anyone who might impugn it. His great history tells in detail of his encounters with misbelievers and disbelievers of all kinds. But, except for King Chilperic, who was an open enemy of the Christian church and a thorn in the bishop's side for many years, none of those who argued doctrine with Gregory were Franks. They were perhaps overawed by the bishop's erudition; it is likely that they had trouble communicating with him for he spoke no Frankish. In any event, Gregory, though well prepared for exciting theological dispute found few Frankish foes worthy of his steel.

Not that he did not have plenty to occupy him as bishop of Tours. He had to discipline the lesser clergy and settle their disputes, had to supervise the cultivation of the church lands, care for the church's property and fabric, defend himself against multiple accusations raised by malice and greed, memorialize the martyrs of faith — all while keeping on good terms with a series of restless and truculent monarchs and their violent wives. Between the Franks and their Roman hosts/ victims/teachers there were many relations of great complexity and unpredictability, that kept both parties busy most of the time and on edge all of the time. But of intellectual community there are few signs.

Clovis came to kingship over the Franks by inheritance from his father Childeric, the son of Merocech, who may have been the son of the obscure Clodio, founder of the line as far as anyone knows. Of the four sons of Clovis among whom his holdings were divided, three were eliminated by war or sickness, leaving Lother sole heir. He also had four sons, two of whom died at the hands of assassins and one of disease, leaving only Guntram to be king. For a Merovingian king, Guntram survived a long time. His father Lothar I died in 561, and Guntram — taking over his brothers' estates as they perished — survived till 593. Undoubtedly his health was extremely robust; in addition, he was a skilled manipulator of alliances, breaker of treaties, and uncoverer of plots. His turbulent sex life kept him well stimulated; his furious uncertain temper kept his royal retainers at a respectful distance. Though he had the misfortune to lose his two sons Lothar and Chlodomer to the dysentery, he named Childbert II (a son of King Sigibert and therefore Guntram's nephew) as his adopted son. And while it would be an exaggeration to describe their relation as tranquil, neither of them in fact killed the other; and in a Merovingian monarchy that was exceptional.

One day while riding with Childebert through the royal game preserve deep in the Vosges mountains, King Guntram made a significant discovery. This was the spoor or trail of an aurochs, and very exciting it was, though one cannot be sure quite why. The aurochs or primitive ox of Europe was a rare and ancient creature. It was also enormous, and some surviving skeletons indicate that it stood an authentic six feet high at the shoulder, with huge horns. But what could one hope to do with this magnificent anachronism? To kill it, cook it, and eat it like a common beef was a destiny unworthy of its immensity, its antiquity. There is no reason to think its meat was particularly tasty; it may well have been tough. Rare it was, but there was no practical way to exhibit it. All such considerations, however, were irrelevant to the present aurochs. He was dead: someone had killed him.

Not surprisingly, King Guntram was furious. Hunting in the royal preserve was forbidden in any case; to kill an aurochs there verged on lèse-majesté. (It is interesting to contrast Guntram's indignation over the killing of the aurochs with his relative equanimity over the assassination of his two brothers and fellow-monarchs, Sigibert (575) and Chilperic (584). The first of these killings may have surprised him less because he himself had ordered his brother killed.) In any case, the aurochs was the present problem; and to find out about his fate, the royal forester was summoned. His story was straightforward, positive, and unwavering; it was also improbable. The killer of the aurochs, he said, was the royal chamberlain (cubicularius), Chundo. Arrested and taken in chains to Chalon-sur-Saone (Cabyllonia), Chundo protested vehemently and at length his total innocence. He did not know who had killed the aurochs; he was positive that he had not done so. As he was in the king's court, he might have asked (we do not know if he did so), when he could have slunk off and killed the aurochs. He might have called on witnesses who had seen him far from the fatal spot. The forester persisted with equal assurance that Chundo was the guilty party. Nobody asked directly if he had witnessed the fatal deed — or if he had, why he did not intervene with Chundo to stop the killing or to threaten the killer with King Guntram's wrath. The two witnesses stood on their unsupported words, and they told exactly opposite stories.

King Guntram, his wits taxed to the utmost, decided to submit the case to the test of trial by combat. Chundo, mistrusting his own skill with sword and spear, asked that a nephew of his do battle in his place. The plea was granted, the combat proclaimed. When it began, the nephew cast a spear at the forester, and nailed one of his feet to the ground. Advancing on his fallen enemy, the nephew undertook to cut his throat; but the forester, writhing on the ground, drew his dagger too, and planted it in the nephew's midriff. In short order they both lay dead.

Chundo, seeing this outcome, understood the consequences for himself, and started running as fast as he could for the church of Saint Marcellus. (Possibly he misinterpreted the outcome of the fight, for if the forester had killed the nephew, by the same token the nephew had killed the forester. Nobody had really won the trial, and if Chundo had stood still, someone might have thought it out. But he ran. It was a confession, or was so interpreted.) Having lost, or failed to win, the battle, his only hope was to take sanctuary somewhere. Guntram and the court ran after him pell-mell, and in the nick of time they caught him. After that the formalities were few and quick. They tied the wretched man to a stake, and threw stones at him till he died, as miserably as it's possible to conceive of a man dying. That's the end of the story.

Afterward there was a lot to think about. Perhaps there always is after an act of summary justice. King Guntram was very sorry, for Chundo had been a faithful servant and a good chamberlain. No doubt the forester had been a good forester too, and the nephew, in defending his uncle's honor, had followed the code. They were all good men, unless Chundo — against all appearances — was a villain and a barefaced liar;

or unless the forester, for no apparent reason at all, was a malicious, unmotivated liar. More likely than either of these alternatives was the notion of a third party, which never came up. The king's preserves were not fenced or guarded; beyond them Teutonic forests stretched away for uncounted miles, to the Baltic and the frozen northland. Possibly some malcontent or dispossessed peasant from Poland or Lithuania — outside the district entirely — had killed the aurochs. Such a vagrant might well have been hungry, and killed for meat. But we do not hear that the aurochs had been cut up for cooking or carried away anywhere. Both the forester and the chamberlain had court employment; they did not need to poach to eat — or if they did, they might have killed a more portable victim — a rabbit or a deer. The killer seems to have made no effort to conceal his deed or the manner of his villainy. We do not know if one man killed the aurochs with a spear, or if several men did it with bows and arrows. We do not know if it was killed an hour or so ago, or last week. If Chundo killed it, one can hardly imagine he would linger around the corpse while the killing was investigated; why didn't he run away? An outsider would have made tracks for home, which might be anywhere; the first place to look for him would be far away.

Somewhere in the story is buried a logic that isn't extinct to this day: someone had killed the aurochs, so someone close to hand (and for some reason visible and identifiable) had to pay the price, right away and in public. The king's dignity would not be salved if all the Frankish warriors had to set off on a long chase after an unknown and perhaps undiscoverable malefactor. Punishment would likely be secret, under those circumstances, and of no exemplary value. Much better to make a state occasion of it, whether one got the right criminal or not. For the crime was not just the killing the aurochs, it was killing the *king's* aurochs. We are not told why the king cared so deeply about the killing of his aurochs; we know nowadays that it was an endangered species, but Guntram would not have known that or cared if he did. If he thought it a precious creature, why didn't he protect it better? The trial by combat might well have gone against the forester; then the only point established would have been Chundo's innocence, and who killed the aurochs would have remained forever unknown. Of course, as things turned out, the killer of the aurochs remained completely unknown anyway; but the atrocious killing of Chundo righted the balance of feeling — a bad act had been done, someone had paid for it, the books could now be closed.

Chundo's position in the court of King Guntram was one of multiple jeopardy. He enjoyed privileges, it is safe to assume, that many people envied and he was not fully able to defend. A chamberlain was a personal attendant to the king, looking out for his creature comforts; occasionally he took a supervisory hand in the royal finances. In the routine of things, he was apparently much more a bureaucrat than a warrior. It is hard to imagine any motive (short of temporary insanity) for Chundo's killing the aurochs. If he was a thief, his ordinary employment gave him access to money and jewels in a thousand forms more convenient and portable than a two-ton ox. In the other direction, the forester's position is a bit more doubtful. If he had struck a deal with a hypothetical gang of poachers, pinning the guilt on Chundo would remove suspicion from the forester (nobody could expect him to guard against high officers of the king's own court), while providing an admirably visible scapegoat. He might have counted on Chundo's inability or unwillingness to undergo ordeal by battle. Allowing the more dangerous nephew to fight in his uncle's behalf may have been what queered the forester's pitch. (And, in passing, who decided (as if we didn't know) that it was all right for Chundo to undergo trial by combat through a proxy? Isn't the point of this ancient institution that god is supposed to favor the innocent party? What sort of innocence could be imputed to Chundo from the fact that his nephew happened to be a better fighter than the forester? Suppose he had several nephews and chose (as in prudence he would) to be represented by the most muscular. Wouldn't that in some measure tip the scales of divine justice? But these are complexities which never occurred to the court considering Chundo's case, for the very good reason that, as far as we can tell, there was no such court).

Apart from the aurochs himself (who constituted a standing invitation to trouble simply by wandering around the forest, an object of great value, deeply tabooed yet almost wholly unprotected), the agency most at fault may have been the law. The Salic law was indeed in existence, and might have been consulted by men learned in the law. But its location was as obscure as its language; it said nothing about aurochses, or about actions for trespass. Even though there was nothing written in the ancient codex, let alone promulgated across the countryside, Chundo and the forester might have known, because of their proximity to the court, that this was a dangerous beast, not to be interfered with. But peasants and serfs, not to speak of travellers from outside the Frankish realm, could only guess. Perhaps one such outsider, or a group of them, simply guessed wrong, fled the countryside, and left King Guntram to vent his rage on the people nearest to hand.

Here we come up against a problem that it's surely too pretentious to call one of jurisdiction, though it touches on those troubled matters. Guntram was king of the Franks, for sure, but did he also wield authority over foreigners, outsiders, and transients passing through Frankish territory, specifically the royal game preserves? He certainly assumed so; he would have stared and snorted had the question ever been raised before him. But he did little or nothing to publish his rules and regulations along the forest trails in the different languages that foreigners might be expected to understand. No doubt that was too much to expect; but evidently Frankish impatience of fixed boundaries had its troublesome side.

Again, the Franks made trouble for themselves by having so limited a gamut of procedures for discovering the truth or falsity of judicial testimony. Short of mortal combat, which was always readily available, dozens of ways to reach a decision lay close at hand. For example, one could cast lots or invite the contestants to swear on the tomb of a particularly active saint (Denis and Martin were favorites) or one might consult a highly charged text like Virgil or the Bible. But none of these alternatives, or others which could have been devised were considered even momentarily in the case of Chundo. The decision to have the two parties fight it out was the king's personal choice. To be sure, it was not a very fair arrangement, as the king himself admitted when he granted Chundo the right to be represented by his nephew. The idea was to have a fair fight, in which the influence of the god of battles might prevail; if one combatant was distinctly better than the other, the result would not be a trial but an execution. Still, trial by combat was the manly procedure, and with the adjustment indicated, it went forward.

A patient criminal investigator, assigned to what could be called the aurochs case, (such an investigator is of course imaginary) would have had a wide range of matters to look into. Her might have begun by examining, or getting a report on, the wounds on the body of the aurochs. From them he could have learned, at least, if the assault had been the work of a single attacker or of a group of malefactors. Since the aurochs had left a spoor (specifically that by which Guntram and Childebert traced him), it might be followed out till one knew where he had come from. (A hazard might be that he would turn out not to be the king's aurochs at all.) Or one might find where his killer or killers had come from. Both Chundo and the forester must have left footprints; by studying them, one might learn which of the men had been stalking the great beast. Tracks on the forest floor might even show where each man had been standing when the might creature met his death. Perhaps (one might learn) several sets of travellers had passed along the trail in addition to Chundo. The more one investigated the evidence, the more possibilities might be expected to emerge. As it was, the procedure of the Franks narrowed down the question of the auroch's death to an absolute minimum — either Chundo killed him or there was no knowing who did. (Suspicion never lighted on the forester himself, though perhaps it should have. Maybe the forester aspired to the easier and doubtless more lucrative post held by Chundo, and hoped, by framing him, to get it. Would he in fact have been eligible for it? Again, we do not know.)

These questions, and many others like them, the Franks never investigated. Why not? Partly, no doubt, because they were incurious and unimaginative. They did not have a cadre of professional investigators whose professional advancement and financial well-being depended on thinking up alternative explanations of crime. If anything, the technicalities of evidence and legal rules bored them. Their impatience to have a controversy out in straightforward man-to-man fight was not just bloody-mindedness; they were not lawyers, they were warriors first and foremost — the legal technicalities came hard to them. No doubt state business like treaties and boundary definitions had to be executed with all the formalities, but it was heavy going. Besides, it cannot be said that even the highest authorities in the land set a very good example of following the law, supposing it could be found.

Could one even describe in legal language the process by which King Clovis (of the Salic branch) acquired territories previously held by the Ripuarian branch of the Franks? As the sons of Childeric, Clovis and Sigibert divided their father's estate, Clovis taking one branch, Sigibert the other. (This was Sigibert the Lame in consequence of his efforts at battle of Chalons; his son, and consequently Clovis's nephew, was Chlodoric.) Peace prevailed in the family till one day Clovis wrote from Paris to his nephew, intimating that brother Sigibert was old and unwell, and that if he should die Chlodoric would succeed him — adding, to remove the last ambiguity, that in that unfortunate event, the friendship of Clovis would come with the young king's new inheritance. Such a hint was quite enough. Chlodoric took a convenient occasion to have his father murdered, and then wrote to his uncle, Clovis, inviting him to come and take what he wanted from the treasure chest of his late brother Sigibert. Clovis replied with proper unction that such a distribution would not look good and might give rise to talk; that he would send envoys to look over the treasure, but could not accept any of it for himself. The envoys came and were duly shown into the treasury; they admired the trunk full of gold coins, and invited Chlodoric to sink his arm into the hoard to show how deep it was. He reached in up to his elbow, and while he was thus bent over, one of the envoys split his skull with a battle axe. In short order Clovis appeared on the scene to deplore the murders of Sigibert and Chlodoric, the second of which he attributed to unknown parties. But since the deplorable deeds had now been done, he suggested that the Ripuarian Franks could do no better than accept his protection. They gladly did so, and Clovis with equal gladness accepted their generous offer, along with the gold.

Whether any of this actually happened, or in the way we hear of it from the only historian of the age we possess, nobody can or should feel very positive. Clovis presents Gregory with a particularly difficult problem in royal portraiture. He is a king, a maintainer of the dynasty, a mighty warrior, an admirably successful fellow. Yet there is not much good to be said of his family relations. Within three pages of his murdering Sigibert and Chlodoric (p. 155), he is found bewailing his loneliness, his utter lack of kinfolk. "How sad a thing it is that I live among strangers like some solitary pilgrim and that I have none of my own relations left to help me when disaster threatens." (p. 158). Gregory does not venture to point out that the solitude of the melancholy monarch was very much of his own making. The limit of the bishop's audacity is the suggestion that Clovis may have been trying, by his pathetic lament, to lure a few last relations out of hiding so that he could kill them too. Yet the kings are mostly fine fellows, and Gregory does not venture to express the summary condemnation that he must surely have felt.

For his own safety's sake, Gregory was well advised to write of the Frankish kings in the optative mood — as he would have liked them to be, not as they were. His subjects were to be feared as much as the king himself. Guntram's subjects viewed their lord rather as a saint, and preserved scraps of his discarded clothing as holy relics (p.150). Their reverence for the monarch was much like his own. Like most of the Frankish kings, he was in fact a man of deep suspicions and hair-trigger temper. As his second wife the king married Marcatrude, daughter of King Magnachar. Once installed, she took the wise precaution of poison

---

Page numbers: *"The History of the Franks"* by Gregory of Tour

ing Gundobad, Guntram's son by an earlier mistress, Veneranda. Shortly thereafter Marcatrude was estranged from Guntram, who sent her away to some place where she conveniently died. The brothers of Marcatrude, sons of the now-deceased Magnachar, ventured to speak slightingly of the good king's third wife, Austrechild — whereupon, he had both of them executed. Whatever they said had evidently been too much; had they said nothing at all, that also would have been too much. Their silence would have been proof that they were thinking unacceptable thoughts. Perhaps only a clinical psychiatrist (if such had been available) could have explained some royal decisions. Magnovald was an unremarked attendant at the court of Childebert. One day when the king was watching the baiting of some animal at the arena, he summoned Magnovald. The retainer watched the action for some minutes and then without warning had his skull split open by a servant or bystander wielding the familiar battle-axe. Perhaps Magnovald had murdered his wife in order to sleep undisturbed with his deceased brother's wife; likely he had. But in the Frankish social scale, that was not much of a crime; and if it was a crime, surely the church was responsible for looking into it. Perhaps Magnovald had been suspiciously absent from one beast-baiting too many; perhaps he was suspected of reading a book or of finding the court entertainments boring. All we know is that his body was thrown out of the window, and his men buried it. What did they grumble as they carried off the carrion?

Some ways down the social scale the same pattern of hideous passions suddenly emerging makes itself felt. Sichar and Chramensind, citizens of Tours, got into a violent quarrel at a Christmas party (pp. 428, 501 ff.). The bishop, who was Gregory himself, and the judge or judges in the city, got involved. Swords were drawn, in the end to fatal effect, and fines were levied. Lest any of the parties be seriously inconvenienced, Gregory offered the resources of the church to meet the payments. Admittedly this generous arrangement was against the letter of the law, but the bishop promoted the formula as a way of negotiating peace. And so, for the moment, it turned out. The rivals were reconciled and good will of a sort prevailed, for a while. Fines were paid, oaths sworn, and the two principals became intimate friends. They fraternized, took meals together, occasionally slept in the same bed. One day Chramensind invited Sichar to supper, and they sat long over their wine. Sichar got carried away, and told Chramensind gaily that the fines he (Sichar) had had to pay as a result of their previous quarrel were the reason Chramensind was now a rich man. He dwelt at some length on this topic, not to his friend's unalloyed content. Sichar suspected nothing, but babbled on till he put himself to sleep. Chramensind, fuming with suppressed resentment and shame over his own failure to stand by his kinfolk, rose from the table quietly, got his ever-handy axe, and split his friend's skull as he lay snoring. Then he stripped the corpse and hung it on a post of his garden-fence, perhaps with the implication that this is how one treats vermin.

The murderer went immediately to see King Childebert, and told him the whole story. It was the king's decision that if Chramensind could prove that he killed to avenge an insult, he could go free. Childebert's queen, Brunhild, might have interfered with the judgement, and tried to do so, not on proper legal grounds exactly, just because Sichar had been "her" man; but the king's decision stood. The only person who might have contradicted Chramensind's story was, as it happened, dead. (A modern quibbleweaver would have had no difficulty in setting forth the argument that Sichar, being blind drunk, could not have formed the fixed intention of insulting Chramensind; but such legal refinements were unthought of in the 6th century.) In any case, the murderer returned to the monarch, got back most of the money he had forfeited, profited by the fact that Queen Brunhild was busy for the moment with another set of problems, and settled down to a new life. Meanwhile, Sichar's widow found a new fellow and moved in with him. Gregory gives us clearly to understand that he did not think Sichar much of a loss.

Nobody in the 6th century seems to have defined what it meant exactly, to be "the queen's" or "the king's man." But to the Frank it clearly meant something specific and real. And it modifies sharply our sense of the predictability of the law at that period of history. Being "someone's man" could mean something like immunity from judicial prosecution; it could also mean something much less pleasant. A young couple in the service of Duke Rauching had the misfortune to fall in love and get married. Not because he disapproved of what they had done, nor that they had done it without his permission, but apparently from sheer meanness, the duke had them shut up in a hollow log and buried alive. The local clergyman protested as much as he dared, and with some difficulty the wretched couple was dug up — but too late to save the girl. The duke seems to have thought it a great joke — they were, after all, his people (256).

Clerics were, as a rule, a little more mildly treated than laymen. The two brothers Salonius and Sagittarius ran most of the disciplinary gamut. They were appointed bishops when relatively young (one bishop of Embrun, the other of Gap), but then proceeded to behave not only like laymen but like particularly rowdy laymen. They fought in battles, killing enemy soldiers when they could, they consorted with loose women, laid violent hands on their neighbors' property, and assaulted the venerable Victor of Saint-Paul-Trois-Chateaux. By vote of a commission of their fellow bishops, the two rogues were deposed, but they persuaded King Guntram, obviously a kindred soul, to plead with Pope John for their reinstatement. By then their joint careers of crime were barely begun. Another assemblage of bishops found them guilty of adultery and murder, but allowed them to purge themselves by penitence, i.e. by saying they were sorry. However, charges of high treason and lèse majesté were added to the bill, and as these affected the dignity of the monarch, the two scoundrels were shut up in a monastery. But before long they were liberated, and then turned loose to wander the countryside. Salonius disappears from sight as a common vagabond, but his brother Sagittarius achieved a more spectacular conclusion. Drawn inevitably to forlorn causes, he took up that of the Pretender Gundovald. In the general massacre which followed the murder of that adventurer, Sagittarius tried to conceal his episcopal appearance, or what was left of it, and skulk off the battlefield. Whether he was recognized and killed because he was Sagittarius, or not recognized and killed on general principles is historically moot, but he was thoroughly decapitated.

Such, such was a sampling of the ways of Frankish society in the early middle ages. There is no reason to be surprised if the law — though present in many different manifestations — never struck very deep roots in the actual procedures of the community. The social groups assigned to enforce different parts of the law (bishops and royal retainers) were themselves criminals, murderers, scalawags, and irresponsible scoundrels. Gregory does not propose that the state of public affairs in his part of Gaul was scandalous; over the years he quietly takes for granted that things were very much that way. His position naturally called on him to take notice of disorders and disturbances and in that sense he doubtless exaggerated, as a daily newspaper does today when it neglects 364 uneventful days in the life of a community to highlight one day of atrocities and lawless mayhem.

But if Gaul was lawless from top to bottom, as the report suggests, the problem of who killed the aurochs is not only insoluble, it is unimportant. Any rough vagabond or momentary group of vagabonds could have done it. One need only be strong enough, malicious enough, and favored by a bit of secrecy, of which the Vosges had plenty. The first solid guess has to be that Chundo did *not* do it. He was not strong enough, he was too conspicuous, he had no positive motivation, he had a position to lose. The man who avoided fighting the forester would not have attacked the aurochs single-handed, or if he did the marks of struggle would have been on him. Against the basic first principle of most such investigations, I think the search for the killer of the aurochs ought to begin at a generous remove from the site of the crime. The aurochs himself was a transient rarity in Guntram's realm; he came from outside Gaul, from the very edges of Europe; perhaps his murderer did too.

Historians might well label this period of time by a name which would have sounded strangely in the ears of participants — the Breaking of Nations. The Teutonic inhabitants of modern Poland, Lithuania, Yugoslavia, and Prussia were all on the move, under pressure from Goths and beyond them Huns; the clans were compressed, fractured, and pushed vaguely westward to struggle with earlier settlers. People were on the move, and so were their flocks or at least the cattle they used to supervise. Communities were everywhere shattered and dispersed. The aurochs was just as much of a displaced person as the Cimbri and Alamanni or perhaps the hypothetical killer of the animal.

The Franks, who had experienced their own form of nomadic wandering a little earlier, were by the fifth century entering a stage of settling down. In a couple of generations more, they would be solidifying into an established empire under Charlemagne. However chaotic things looked under the likes of Guntram and Childebert, they were developing toward a central administration, a written code of established laws, a rule of predictable order. They would have books then, and scholars to read the books, and libraries to catalogue them. In the terrible process of drumming order into the tribes (friends and foes alike, as if they could be distinguished), Chundo was an agent and, as it happened, a victim. We need not feel sorry for him; he was a vulnerable component of a bureaucracy that many people had good reason to hate — and that would still be hated twelve hundred years later when they wore lace at their wrists, wigs on their heads, and thought a dozen eggs was about enough to make an omelet for one man.

◆

# II A SET OF LETTERS

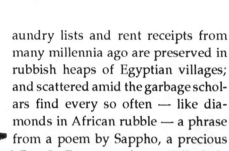

aundry lists and rent receipts from many millennia ago are preserved in rubbish heaps of Egyptian villages; and scattered amid the garbage scholars find every so often — like diamonds in African rubble — a phrase from a poem by Sappho, a precious line by Philetas of Cos. In Europe and especially Italy there is just as much inert material — called trash or junk only by those who do not grasp what treasures it contains. To uncover the four precious documents here made public required the devoted efforts of dozens of scholars, antiquarians, translators, and interpreters — not to speak of an enormous computer network for searching through the garbage middens of the peninsula. The society of associated serendipidists was also of immense assistance. To all cooperating scholars and generously supportive institutions, the editor expresses his gratitude.

The letters from Lorenzo, Stultitia, and the Cardinal d'Este appeared in the *Virginia Quarterly* for Spring 1974; the letter of Count Lodovico Michelini, whose pneumatic temperament relates him to the family of tire-manufacturers, appeared in *Sewanee Review* for Spring, 1984.

*Count Lodovico Michelini*

*to the Countess Angelina Buonsignori at Lucca*

August 1638, Florence

Darling:

Need I tell you how you've been missed this season at Florence? Of course I don't need to, but I tell you anyway. Life here without you has been as dreary as — well, let's see — as a dinner without wine or a carnival without songs or a race without a bet. I'm sorry that these are all trite and stupid comparisons. I'd have recourse to the poets, but you'd instantly recognize the superiority of Messer Francesco's fancy to mine — and what would I get for my pains but the reputation of a plagiarist to sit atop my reputation as a rake, like a dunce's cap on a condemned thief? One vice at a time is my motto — or, at the most three. I indulge in none when I tell you simply that your company has been missed, and of all the sad, dull dogs about town, none has been sadder and duller than your humble servant.

Why do husbands get gout in the first place? We should organize a conference on the topic, with all parties represented. I challenge you to show me a gouty lover. Obviously they have to be so nimble and versatile, what with singing and rhyming and dancing and picking up handkerchiefs and carrying shawls, that the disease hasn't time to lay hold of them. Whereas, husbands . . . but if they have to get the gout, and apparently they have to, why can't they take the cure by themselves where they can provide good dumpish company for one another while their wives, bubbling with good health and good spirits, enjoy the harmless diversions of the town and the court? I daresay you've made these reflections yourself, and perhaps conveyed them to your lucky gentleman directly — to no avail, as we sense all too painfully from one end of this forlorn town to the other. As for your state, I can prophesy.

You drink the waters and promenade morning and afternoon on the walks; you talk scandal and play cards and are mightily bored — oh, I know the whole routine, because my father was a regular visitor to the baths after his younger diversions became too strenuous for him. Heigh-ho! What an estimable gentleman, you husband; I really do wish he'd get better, and bring you back to town. Failing that, a decisive step in the other direction would also be welcome, returning you to us as a bouncing and flourishing widow - I think we could make the period of your mourning pass very agreeably indeed.

Meanwhile you are there where there's no news, and we are here where there's very little, so I must entertain you with what we have. Politics is of course at a complete standstill, since there are only two sorts of opinion at court, the impeccably correct and abominably dull. Ferdinand is the same kind, gentle, henpecked person he's always been, and I'm sure it would distress him no end to rack a suspected traitor, or sentence him to thirty years in the galleys. But on the other hand he's a well-trained monarch who would never think of shirking his duties, however painful. So we all profess sentiments of amazing correctness, three times a day a after meals. God be thanked, there are no wars afoot in which our loyalty might have to be put to the test. Not that it isn't perfectly sincere and honorable, as far as it goes — just that if there's one thing history has taught us, it's that we Florentines don't make very good soldiers. Ferdinand has learned that too, or knew it to begin with — God be thanked, he's a true Medici, not a swashbuckling sword rattler like that savage Giovanni delle Bande Nere for instance. Consequently we jog along comfortably enough. Corn, wool, oil, wine, and money are often in short supply; on the other hand we are blessed with a generous crop of priests sprinkled among us by the Holy Father in his paternal wisdom. We count them among our temporal and spiritual blessing, and have to keep counting because every day there are more of them. Popular opinion says they are all nephews and cousins of the Pope, but I assure you this is a gross and slanderous exaggeration. Only the other day I spoke with one of them, and he assured me he was no kin whatever — *barbarous*, yes, he said, but not *Barberini*.

Lacking serious business, we've occupied ourselves with meetings of the academies, generally under the leadership of Don Lorenzo, who fancies himself a universal scholar. (There's a good side to this ambition, since he regularly compounds his own medications, and as a result is often too sick to take part in the conferences he arranges.) We've had some quite amusing sessions, the formula being very nicely established now — that there's not to be too much heavy learning ( a rule made for the benefit of people like me), and on the other hand not a complete diet of social chitchat (which would distress the six or seven academicians who really know something). Sometimes we have a single speaker, sometimes a panel discussion, very occasionally a debate of some sort. (But most people find the debates too stimulating: they also have a distressing way of wandering in the direction of forbidden topics, so we don't have many of them.) There's always a bit of music, an agreeable snack, a glass or two of wine — it's a pleasant way to get through an afternoon, when the weather isn't too sultry.

And, of course, we never know exactly what the day's program will be. We may hear from one of our own, or from a visiting scholar, passing through on his way to Rome; we may have a singer on her way to fill an engagement at Parma or Venice. In fact the other week we had just such a pair. The scholar was, to our surprise, a quite young man from England, of all places: Signor Giovanni Miltone, if you please, of London city — untitled, unbeneficed, a graduate of their university but holding no appointment there. Simply a young man of some wealth and some scholarly attainments, traveling alone in Italy to complete his education. The singer was Leonora, the soprano of whom you've surely heard, on her way to do a series of concerts with Pre Monteverdi in Venice. Because I was forlorn over your absence, and because I'd known Leonora a bit many years ago in Rome, I was asked to serve as her escort. Young Miltone made a show of being interested in the stars, though he also carries the name of a poet, so finding someone to introduce him wasn't easy: they finally picked old Signor Aggiunti who I think once wrote something on the Latin poet-astronomer Manilius. In any case, he's now very feeble and stone-deaf, so out of sheer pity for young Miltone I rubbed up an acquaintance with him, and got to know him a bit.

He came with excellent recommendations from England, and some letters from friends in the north; yet I must confess — when we first heard of him we all expected a monster of some sort. He's a heretic, of course, as they all are up there; and we couldn't suppose he'd had much exposure to good learning, or for that matter to good manners. And it seemed ridiculous to suppose that he would know decent Latin, far less understandable Italian. After all, he was, as we were told, less than thirty years old, and what should he have picked up in that climate, in those surroundings? If he had picked up anything, why didn't he have an office, an appointment, a position? At worst we thought he would be a young boar like Martin Luther — more likely a callow cub in need of some licking. How wrong we were!

A slender, modest young man, quite handsome though a little pale by our standards; white skin, gray eyes not very strong — the eyes of a bookman, not an athlete. But still, an erect figure and good shoulders. The Latin superb; Italian very adequate, though his pronunciation in both tongues seemed odd to us. But he reads and speaks Greek too, and (he confessed), some Hebrew. God knows what else — probably some six or eight more tongues as well. We never dared ask about his Arabic or his Transylvanian. He's a heretic, undoubtedly: there was a moment when he stared at the Cardinal as if expecting horns and hooves — but a close-mouthed, well-spoken heretic. Not a word of divinity could we get out of him; he knew the controversialists, knew the names of all their books, smiled a little smile and said — nothing. I asked where he learned his Italian, and it seems he knew some of the Diodati family who left Florence because of religion — it must have been long before your time. But his Latin and all those other languages he must have learned in the English schools. And not just the languages — the books he's read in them! Why it's positively frightening. Some of our graybeards tried him out on the historians; he was extremely polite, but it was perfectly apparent that he knew Sallust and Ammianus Marcellinus and the least of the *Scriptores Historiae Augustae* forwards and backwards — better than any of them. One of them quoted a passage to him; he corrected the text according to the newest emendations. My old friend Luciano tried him on Martial and Propertius (he's made a special study of the erotica): same story. The Greek tragedians, the modern political writers, natural history, the art of war, Sannazaro, Longinus, Poliziano, Prudentius, Vitruvius, Columella. He wasn't smart or showy: you could tell he wasn't pushing the conversation into areas where he could shine. He let other people take the lead, and where they led he followed; but my God, the different things he knew would make your head spin. What was most impressive was the sense of reserve. Divinity was out of bounds, and so, for different reasons, was the recent history of northern countries; but it was clear he could have talked on textual criticism of the Bible or the Council of Trent as well and as long as he did on Cato of Utica and Ariosto. Good manners, too: no awkward pauses. I will say he didn't seem overgifted with a sense of humor, but there were reasons for that. If I were his age, the only foreigner in an English Academy, and speaking a foreign language, I daresay my wit wouldn't be exactly sparkling.

In short our Signor Miltone was a prodigious success even before he'd pronounced his formal allocution in front of the academy. And you can imagine, perhaps, that Leonora the singer was not altogether delighted with his success. Singers are all alike: any three minute period that passes without a compliment on their divine voice or their ravishing beauty is, for them, three minutes lost. And Leonora is one of the worst in this way. Once I told her, she sang divinely, and she said "Is that all?" Nothing less than a half-hour oration would satisfy her. Oh, most of the people at this particular gathering didn't notice, but I could tell by the glassiness of her smile, the rhythm of her fan, that she'd had about enough. So I drew her aside, out of sheer politeness, you understand; plied her with flattery, distracted her attention; and after a while, between jest and earnest, what began as simply a catty remark on her part developed into a serious wager between us. She proposed to seduce young Signor Miltone within the next twenty-four hours; I wagered that enamel brooch which has been a family possession for years and years (the one with Medusa's head in the center) that she couldn't do it.

A curious affair, right? Yet I was bored and she was spiteful. Neither of us had ever laid eyes on the young man before, but there was vanity involved, on my side as well as hers. I do rather pride myself on being a judge of human nature, at least that aspect of human nature. Oh, there are a thousand little signs — no need to remind you! — that can be read in the movement of a man's eyes, the set of his shoulders, the softening of his voice. Leonora could read them as well as I could: Lord knows she's had plenty of practice. But I think she saw him as a challenge; and of course he'd piqued her vanity. Actually it was a one-way bet as far as I was concerned. She got the brooch if she succeeded with him, I got nothing whether she succeeded or failed — except the pleasure of the comedy, which believe me, was reward enough.

For I was pretty sure of my man. Not that he was insensible, since he was certainly far from unattractive; and something about the lips suggested a natural, though latent, talent. And yet I don't know — the eyes, the bearing, the very perfection of his control, suggested to me that we had with us a *casto Giuseppe*. Why do we make these guesses, how do we know? Nothing but an accumulation of nothings, yet somehow when we put them together we can feel certain, or almost certain — unless spite or vanity blinds us. And so I thought it was with my poor unfortunate Leonora.

She had some things in her favor, I admit. A splendid figure, not quite as dazzling as it was a few years ago before she overdeveloped it, but still impressive. A flashing eye, a torrent of dark hair, a commanding presences, a theatrical wardrobe — plus of course her voice. Quite a spectacular voice it is; and she has the temperament to go with it. Though she looks a little like Bradamante, she sings like Angelica, and she's at her very best in those warm, melting, ambiguous songs to which our liquid language lends itself so well. Besides she and Signor Miltone were staying at the same inn — where else but Signor Bevigliano's Chiavi d'Oro? And young Miltone is not only a poet, but something of a musician . . . so there were reasons enough for Leonora's confidence. In fact there were sporting chances on both sides, and say what you will about Leonora (I know you've never liked her), she's a girl who relishes a sporting chance.

All these arrangements and calculations occupied the first part of the afternoon; and then, after Don Lorenzo arrived, we adjourned to the meeting room for the more formal part of the program. Young Ser Giovanni was to talk on the music of the spheres, after which we would have samples of the same by Leonora — rather neat, eh? And so afterwards the customary colazione and adjournment, each to his or her own devices.

The speech was . . . well, apart from the fact that it went very well, and was obviously very learned, I can't tell you much about it. First of all, though I know Latin the way we all know it, I'd never heard it spoken with an English accent, and the vocabulary of astronomy isn't really familiar to me, and frankly I didn't get most of it. He spoke extempore, which was remarkable in itself; he cited Homer and Plato and a hundred other authorities; he quoted long passages of the poets — and from memory; he was ( as far as I could judge) more ingenious than witty, and more learned than ingenious. And then, if I understood correctly, toward the end of the speech he began to suggest, quite indirectly, that the whole subject was nothing but an intricate, charming, empty trifle, a fantasy of the poets. What struck me (but then, as I needn't tell you, I'm no scholar) was why, if he didn't believe in the music of the spheres, he had learned such a fearful lot about it. He'd read more books about the music of the spheres, in which he didn't believe, than I've read about green noodles and *vino nobile*, in which I do most devoutly believe. Well there's scholarship for you — the learned men take you on a long painful perambulation about the nature of something, only to conclude that it never existed in the first place. If he'd started with the last part of his talk, he'd never have needed to drag us through the first part. I daresay that shows why I'm not a scholar and never will be — but doesn't it make sense to you?

In any case the other reason why I didn't do justice to the talk (and it *was* elegant, everyone said the Latin was as fluent and unforced as if he'd been brought up in the same house as Cicero) was that I was busy watching Leonora. Really you'd have thought the Roman Empire was at stake instead of just an old-fashioned enamel brooch. She sat in the front row, she pulled down her neckline, she laughed at the palest ghost of a joke, and she stared at Ser Giovanni as if she expected to eat him for supper that night — which, after a manner of speaking, she really did. The fellow could hardly have failed to notice her, especially when she led the round of applause after he had done, and pushed forward to congratulate him. But he held countenance very well, and kept the conversation general. Here and there some of the sharper young people noticed that something was up, and gave me half a glance, which I confirmed with a quarter of another. So that before long we had a little playlet arranged, with one understanding audience, one completely unsuspecting audience, one actress who knew the script, and an actor the most innocent and unsuspecting you ever saw. By the rules of the game, of course, everything had to be absolutely smooth, socially — and it was. Nobody outside the game suspected for an instant that it was going on; nobody inside said a word or made a gesture that didn't have a hidden meaning. As a troupe of comedians, the half-dozen or so of us who put on the play — *all' improvviso*, mind you — really earned thunderous applause that day. Alas that we can never hope to hear it — alas, too, that you weren't there, my dear, to help us carry it off.

Leonora sang for us. She does have a splendid voice — I'm sorry to repeat myself, but it's true — and she was absolutely in top form. Some of the things she sang I had never heard before, they were by this Venetian Pre' Monteverdi: and though she had only a harpsichord and a viola to accompany her, one could guess from that what they would be like with a full chorus and orchestra. Until the very end she sang without taking any special notice of Signor Miltone, though I must say he seemed as attentive to her as she had been to him — almost. But her last song she addressed directly to him; and since I was particularly taken with it, I took pains to get a copy of the lyrics later. They're really quite polished, after the fashion of Signor Marini and his friends; and as you'll note, they make a particular point of leaving the hearer uncertain whether the singer is perishing of divine love or of some humbler, earthier affliction. Leonora sang the song with her full assortment of runs, divisions, and trills; she directed it squarely at our hero: she practically laid it and herself at Signor Miltone's feet:

> *Love, when the sense of thy sweet grace*
> *Sends up my soul to seek thy face,*
> *Thy blessèd eyes breed such desire*
> *I die in Love's delicious fire*
>     *O Love, I am thy sacrifice;*
> *Be still triumphant, blessèd eyes!*
> *Still shine on me, fair suns! that I*
> *Still may behold, though still I die.*
>
> *Though still I die, I live again,*
> *Still longing so to be still slain;*
> *So gainful is such loss of breath,*
> *I die even in desire of death.*
>     *Still live in me this loving strife*
> *Of living death and dying life.*
> *For while thou sweetly slayest me,*
> *Dead to myself, I live in thee.*

Naturally that was the climax of the occasion. There was enough applause to restore Leonora's self-esteem, even if she hadn't thought herself in a way to winning her bet — as, from the redness of young Ser Giovanni's cheeks, she must certainly have supposed. I'm afraid we who were in the secret in any degree had to be careful not to look one another in the eye. The shadow of a smile, the merest hint of laughter, would have given everything away. I must say, my dear Countess, it's not very often that I've seen love made under such public circumstances, and so openly, at least on one part. The suppressed smile, the private murmur, the foot secretly pressed under the table, even the chit of paper passed discreetly from hand to hand, I believe we've heard of such things, eh? But the charm of this scene was that it was so open to those who guessed, and so closed to those who didn't, as if the onlookers were wearing two absolutely different sets of glasses.

After the performances we adjourned for small talk around the refreshment table; and i assure you that Leonora didn't fail to follow up her advantage. Without being indiscreet about it, I listened nearby, and managed to hear her arrange for him to discover with delight that they were both staying at the Chiavi d'Oro; I noted the grace with which she turned the subject to words, music, and the art of wedding them together; and I was not far away (looking over the convenient screen of someone else's shoulder) when she offered to let him inspect the score of her last song. I even caught a glimpse in a mirror of the very instant when she passed him the rolled-up score of her song, with the key to her room at the inn concealed inside it. Ah, but it was neatly done; really it made me proud of my countrywoman; and I confess, for the first time all afternoon I felt some concern for the safety of my family's brooch. Its real value is rather slight, but I should be sorry to part with it, and even more sorry to be embarrassed in a manner involving my judgement of human character.

In the press of people around the table I momentarily lost sight of my man; I assumed, naturally, that he had pocketed the key, as any other lucky young man would do, in expectation of making use of it later that evening. But suddenly he came straight up to me, and I saw that he was still holding it. He addressed me directly, he had a request to make of me, and I am sure in a thousand years you will never guess what he wanted. What he held in his hand, you understand, was a key to the seventh heaven, a golden key in literal fact; and what he wanted to know was whether I could take him that evening to visit old Galileo, the blind astronomer. Since all his troubles with the holy office, the old man lives in retirement, not far from me on the Costa San Giorgio; seventy-five years old, if he's a day, blind as a mole — and worse than that, a man of the most dangerous reputation conceivable. Twice he's been before the Holy Office, he's under a ban forbidding him to publish, he isn't even supposed to have visitors, and that's where my young man wanted to go! If it's known when he visits Rome that he's been in communication with Galileo, he could suffer a serious misfortune. An Englishman is a

heretic, that's well known, and he could easily be excused a few indiscreet words in a private conversation; but to go out of his way to talk secretly with Galileo! And when he held in his hand the key to a memorable evening of a very different sort! I was actually too dumbfounded to answer him at all, and in my amazement all I could do was stare at the key in his hand. My look reminded him. "Oh yes," he said perfectly calmly, "oh yes, Signorina Leonora has made a little mistake; she will be missing this." And he turned to where she was standing at the center of a dozen other people, made a very pretty bow and a pretty phrase, and handed the key back to her. In public! Before a group of friends and admirers! And do you know something I don't think he did it out of malice, not at all; in innocence, rather, pure and shining innocence. I was staggered before that he knew so much at the age of thirty; this time I was staggered that he knew so little.

Leonora put her best face on it, you may suppose; but a couple of times in the few minutes I stayed at the reception, I caught her looking at our young Englishman as you'd look at a young reptile. For my part, after I recovered from my surprise, I was overflowing with good will toward the man of virtue who'd won my bet for me. Since that was what he wanted, I carried him off at once to see Galileo. It wasn't, let me tell you, the social occasion I would have preferred above all others: in fact it was a fearful bore, with the added possibility of getting myself in serious trouble with the authorities. The pair of them were thick as thieves, talking stars and sunspots and men-in-the-moon and telescopes till my head spun. (By the by Galileo didn't put any stock in the music of the spheres either — simply snorted and laughed at the idea.) For all I know, they were talking heresy — if so, heresy is less dangerous than we've been told, because people will be stupefied long before they are seduced by it. So I let them talk it out, keeping a nervous eye on the street outside for signs of any *sbirri* who might be cruising around the neighborhood.

Afterwards I took young Miltone back to his inn. He was worried, poor fellow, about how to get the score of Leonora's song back to her: I told him not to fret, that I'd take care of it. And just to set her mind at rest, I stopped by a little later in the evening to explain. Having won the bet, I was of a mind to be generous, and I didn't find her in a mood to cherish grudges. As for Ser Giovanni, I plan on giving him letters of introduction to all the librarians I know in Italy, along with a list of the best monasteries to be visited. He'll have a splendid tour.

You know, watching him talk with old Galileo, I couldn't help thinking that I was in the presence of two remarkable men, perhaps the most remarkable I will ever know in my life — yet both blind. My own talent, which is of the commonest sort, has always been for seeing what's under my nose. I used to think poorly of it; now I'm not so sure. In our country, as she is now, what is there for us but to play the comedy? Or maybe our country is what she is now because we are nothing but comedians. Yet even in our comedies we may sometimes show a touch of genius. Do persuade your husband, darling, to bring you back on our Florentine stage, so our comedies may take on again the glitter and inventiveness they once had.

Your sad but hopeful servant,
Lodovico

*Lorenzo, Duke of Urbino, to Niccoló Machiavelli*

May, 1517

My Dear Niccoló,

I received last week the little manuscript you were kind enough to send me, and naturally I've been deeply impressed by it. Your experience in political matters is infinitely greater than my own; and I must say, given the many problems confronting me, my house, and our city, there's nothing from which I could profit more liberally than from your lucid analysis and summary of recent historical experience. Over the years, of course, I'm well aware that we Medici haven't always seen eye to eye with you on particular issues; but as you shrewdly pointed out in one of your later chapters (I think, as a matter of fact, it's number twenty), a prince may well profit most from the advice of one whom he regards, originally, with mistrust.

It's a point very shrewdly proposed, and I have every intention of taking my best advantage of it. But it calls, as I'm sure you'll agree, for a good deal of discrimination. When you argue with such vehemence in your last chapter that I must become the "redeemer" of Italy, that the time is now ripe as never before to throw off the foreign yoke — I seem to be hearing the fervent accents of our late lamented Brother Girolamo. It's noble advice, it's heroic, but I have to ask myself, is it prudent? It seems to me that your own earlier chapters propose a different and much darker analysis of the situation; one which so persuaded me that, frankly, I have some difficulty responding to your final exhortation. I really can't see any way in which the time is ripe for the redemption of our beloved Italy, except on the score that things are already so bad they can hardly get worse. But that's rather like counsel of desperation, isn't it? Your third chapter, which explains in such careful detail how Louis could have held Italy except for a series of egregious, almost ridiculous blunders, seems to me a thoroughly cogent piece of analysis. If he hadn't made six consecutive major errors, you say forcefully, he could have held on to Italy. But if I am now to *redeem* Italy from bondage (a much harder task, as you know), I can't base my policy on the expectation that our opponents, more numerous now and far more powerful than in the days of Louis, will continue to commit the same six stupid blunders. Suppose our little Tuscan-Roman-Medici alliance started to look strong enough to drive the Spaniards out of Italy: just suppose. Wouldn't they immediately seek allies among the Venetians and the Milanese, not to mention our old and bitter enemies in Pisa? Figure it for yourself, Niccoló; all you have to do is look at it from the foreigner's point of view.

I think I understand, and I know I respect, the fervor with which you urge me to become the redeemer of Italy — borrowing, if I'm not mistaken, the exact slogan of Julius II about "driving the barbarians out." But Julius couldn't do it, your old admiration Cesare Borgia couldn't do it. What reason to think I can succeed where these examples — a good deal more immediate, you'll agree, than Cyrus, Theseus, and (of all people!) Moses — were unable to take more than a few halting steps?

No doubt you're thinking that I have the advantage of Uncle Giovanni, whom I still haven't got used to calling His Holiness Pope Leo XIII. Alas, my dear Niccoló, he's the kindest and best of men; and I'm afraid that's why we younger Medici can hardly count on him at all in political matters. He's a true vicar of Christ; I doubt if we will ever see him conniving like that crafty madman Alexander or storming the walls of Bologna like Julius. The church and all true Christians will surely profit by this happy disposition of his; there's no use repining at it. On the other hand, I can't consider him a major source of strength in my campaign (or perhaps I should call it *your* campaign) to liberate Italy from the foreigner.

The other main energy on which you'd have me rely is an army of my own loyal and devoted subjects. Again, it's a wonderful idea, and bound to appear fascinating when one has read as much Livy as I'm told you have. Find me a few hardbitten Roman Republican legions, such as they really had in the days of Cincinnatus, and the reputations of my generals will be made; indeed, I'll be general myself. But my dear fellow, you can't be seriously proposing to build Roman legions out of our Florentine shopkeepers and Tuscan peasants — an army of yardsticks and pitchforks. Tact, I'm afraid, wouldn't allow me to remind you what happened only a few years ago. It was your painfully recruited and instructed militia, wasn't it, that came up against Gonsalvo's veterans before Prato? Well, we won't dwell on that. But as a practical matter of military business — no, Niccoló, it won't work. My Florentines aren't fighters. Not for me, not for Florence, not for the glory that was Rome. When they're at their bravest, they'll put up money to hire someone else to fight for them: that's their manic mood. Generally, they're meek and depressive, and pay over whatever a thug with an army demands as the price of leaving them alone.

For the matter of that, we Medici haven't been much on fighting either. We've always been negotiators, compromisers, balancers, in a city of shopkeepers. What's wrong with that? Nothing, I expect, unless we deceive ourselves into trying to act like Alexander of Macedon or Julius Caesar. The topic is one on which your little book, as I recall, didn't have much to say. The oracle at Delphi was more explicit in two words: Know thyself. That's a saying that you and I could very well contemplate at some length.

When *you* counsel *me* on how to be a prince, there's a good deal involved here besides literature. Let's face it, Niccoló: your training has been as political technician, working for the councils of a republic. I don't downgrade this experience at all; particularly as it's given you the knack of putting political problems in words, it's been of the greatest advantage to you. (And in passing, let me remark how much I've enjoyed your extraordinary gift of style: you tell a story as crisply as Sallust, and some of your aphoristic formulations are so sharp and concise, one would think it was Seneca himself speaking.) Still, there's a good deal in the practice of princecraft that we who are born to it don't think desirable, or even possible, to put into explicit words. And it's just those things that your existential situation (if you'll pardon the pedantry) makes it imperative that you *do* put into words.

Why do you think it necessary, for instance, to tell me that princes don't necessarily keep their word for ever and ever? Apart from the fact that I've read Xenophon's "Cyropaedia" as well as you, don't you suppose that growing up in sixteenth-century Italy has taught me that much at least? Good Heavens, man! Don't you see what happens when you make a formal, conscious rule of policy out of a normal gentlemanly slovenliness with promises which are perfectly understood on both sides as binding only so long as they're for mutual advantage? It's as if we princes slunk about, cackling to ourselves in malign glee every time we broke a treaty. How middle-class can you get? It's not like that at all. From time to time, changing circumstances may make it necessary for one or other of us to change his mind and go back on a previous commitment. But an international treaty isn't like a business contract, Niccoló, really it isn't. One doesn't get sued for breach of contract; one isn't declared a moral bankrupt. It's simply recognized that things have changed, the case is altered. Words can be made to bind people for ever: life changes under the words, we alter the words to conform with the new shapes of life, and wordsmiths call us liars.

As you yourself see and say, Niccoló, we princes are caught between two symbolic systems., one verbal, the other what you might call manipulative. You express this by saying the prince should seem to have all the virtues (in the verbal system of things), but should really exercise them only when they're for his manipulative advantage. When you make this a special rule for princes, and limit the discussion to the practice or non-practice of virtue, you do a number of curious things to the problem, shaping and pointing it in special ways. But in fact, it's a matter of words and things, isn't it? There's a verbal side to government, as to marriage, for example — certain verbal formulas have to be observed. But a whole area of the relationship isn't verbal, and can't be very well expressed in words at all. Ideally, the two system are complementary, but that isn't necessarily so. There are times when all the formulas point one way and all the manipulative realities another — when, in order to achieve substantial real benefit within the relation, one's bound to twist the verbal formulas out of line.

Let me widen the application of these rather obvious ideas by turning them directly toward your little book. You have an ideal verbal system to explain — a set of behavioral rules applying to princes in general, and applying very cleverly as a general thing. But on the manipulative level, your first main task is persuading me personally that you personally are a proper advisor for a prince. Obviously, these two objectives overlap to some extent. But there are also ways in which you've tempered you general advice to advance your personal solicitation. Don't, for Heaven's sake, think I am accusing you of duplicity or bad faith — that would be the most uninteresting figuration of your behavior that could possibly be made. No, it was inherent in the nature of your undertaking that, in order to win my confidence that you knew what you were talking about, you had to write things that a prince in his own person would never think of writing. Put it this way: you tell me that a prince must use hypocrisy — of course he must, and probably more than most men. But the last thing he must do is admit it. With you the case is quite different, and more difficult: you must advocate hypocrisy in the conduct of a prince, but give no sign of practicing it yourself. Once I suspect you of playing the hypocrite with me, the whole game is up.

All this comment points toward the fundamental folly of writing a How-To book on the subject of governing. Every problem a ruler faces is a new one because the complex of objective forces is bound to be new, and even if it's exactly like the preceding complex, it's still new and different, because this is the first time the problem has been faced for a second time. But all How-To books are based on past experience. So in the end you're telling me I should look at the situation overall, consider the peculiar balance of forces involved, and use my best judgement. Thanks a lot, Niccoló.

The reason I'm so conscious of these verbal limitations is, naturally, a social one. I'm perfectly aware that in devising verbal formulas and setting up historical models for imitation, you're a great deal cleverer than I — for all I know, there may be among the secretaries and subsecretaries of the Florentine legations some young fellow who's even cleverer than you. But being clever doesn't make either of you a prince. You'll say, or at least think, that that's what's the matter with princes. I'm not so sure.

Is it really a job for clever, verbal people? In writing an answer to your book, and the problems it poses, you must appreciate that I'm accepting your choice of weapons — which, naturally, I handle (being untrained in their use) only as with my left hand. I have a right-handed answer as well (please don't misunderstand this as a threat); but, for the moment, I'm confident that I can make you see something about the symbolic uses of language by the use of language itself. For this is the crux of the matter. You clever, verbal fellows exist in the medium of words, as we don't; if I may coin another barbarous expression, you're inevitable structuralists, because the value of what you say depends to so large an extent on its coherence, consistency, and logical relatedness. What's an enthymeme or a non-sequitur to you? Everything. What is it to me? A joke. Words for you mean more or less what they say in a neutral, universal context. This is an honorable position, but it's not mine; there's no escaping my *parti pris*. You are judged, among your community of wordsmiths, by your skill at constructing an architecture of words — an architecture which will be judged by your fellow-architects in an atmosphere where I'm afraid the very worst excesses of academic freedom and democracy will prevail. That is, your readers are understood to be sitting in libraries surrounded by books from every period of the world's history; they will be wholly liberated from specific time and concrete circumstances, free from practical distractions but free also from any temptation to apply those painful, exacting tests that we practicing princes have to apply to any discourse. I appreciate that you've done your best to make your little book look practical, not to say "realistic;" and heaven knows, you've come infinitely closer than those medieval fellows whom I've been told to read, but whom I always found much too forbidding and tedious to finish. Since I fell asleep over the moralizings of Egidio Colonna, I simply haven't bothered.

And yet the same taint is on your little book as theirs — it's a book. And a book is, by its inherent nature, democratic, it's the same thing to all men. It implies any context, therefore none. What I want you to see is that the word "prison," dropped casually by me, who have the power to put you there, is not the same thing as it is in your mouth, who haven't been too long out of one. (We're all sorry about that mistake, but on your own view of conspiracies, if I read your Chapter Nineteen correctly, a prince can't be too careful.) The other day I heard a concert given by Uncle Giovanni's choir; it was superb, and really very moving the way the soprani, and above all that excellent fellow Senza Colleoni, sang of love. Yet I couldn't help reflecting on the difference between the word in his mouth, and in yours or mine. We don't warble so nicely, but — well I won't spell it out.

Except when I'm arguing with you, Niccoló, I don't generally use words in a persuasive or discursive way. I don't try to build sequences of thought or learned parallels between myself and the later Roman emperors. Much simpler concepts than that are more complicated than a prince needs, more complicated than he can afford. I've often thought that the real work of a prince could be done, and probably better done than it is now, with just two monosyllables in his mouth. They would be, of course, "Yes" and "No." The prince doesn't need many words because he has another language, which conveys his meanings quite as well, but doesn't commit him to anything, can't be haggled over or questioned. Don't you suppose an ambassador to my court understands precisely, from the clothes I wear when I greet him, the company I place him in, the warmth or coolness of my smile, the subjects I choose to discuss with him (they're all irrelevant to our main business, but significant only as they're congenial or uncongenial) — don't you suppose he understands from all that what I mean to communicate to his master? If he doesn't, he's a pretty poor ambassador.

Thus a prince doesn't have much need of formal discourse at all, and most of us show it in our prose style, which runs (unlike yours) to formulas and ceremonial platitudes. There's an old saying, which I'm afraid hasn't been invented yet, that "Man was given speech in order to conceal his thoughts." For a prince this is particularly true. On half the occasions that confront him, he doesn't want to, and even if he wanted to, couldn't possibly say what he thinks. Because for him speech isn't simply speech, as it is for the ordinary wordsmith, it's a form of action — one of several forms. What he needs most of the time is a neutral formula which lets everything be understood and commits him to nothing. As for example, when, after talking to a group of desperate malcontents, he might say, "I have understood you" — for some reason, it sounds better in French: "Je vous ai compris." Sympathy, sincerity, absolute lack of commitment, incomparable vagueness, unfathomable reservations. Nobody was better at this sort of minimal language than your recent friend Cesare Borgia. Why, the murder of Remirro d'Orco was, all by itself, a piece of moral and political teaching as explicit as anything in Aristotle or Plato. The bloody knife, the piece of stick, the body in two pieces on the snowy square at Cesena, and Christmas morning dawning — oh, it couldn't be bettered as a wordless parable for people to chew and suck and worry during the long winter evenings.

How stiff and formal and inflexible your best rules for princely behavior are, after all! How little room they leave for maneuver and improvisation! To anyone who knows them outside of books, the real complexities of history seem inconceivably remote from the coarse scraps that you can capture in your net of words. And yet your net, Niccolò, is a good deal more finely woven than any that's yet been made. I don't doubt if you made it finer yet, you would capture even more of what you're after — and in the context of a library or scholarly seminar, that might well be one of the most fascinating of intellectual games. Only for a man like me, with a real job of immediate governing to do, it's a toilsome vanity, absorbing me in formulas I don't need, distracting me from realities that are immediate and pressing. When Alexander slashed the Gordian knot, he said something very significant about ruling. Thinkers accept the terms of problems as given and try to solve them; rulers destroy old problems and create new ones.

A curious anomaly in your little book helps to define this relation between words and actions. You begin by distinguishing new states, which are hard to hold, from long-established states, which are easy to hold. This is a good insight, although, as usual, your verbal meshes are too coarse: you surely don't want to exclude the possibility that a regime may become weak, corrupt, or despicable precisely as it becomes old. On the other hand, at the end of the book, you assure me that with wise policies a new prince may become, in short order, just like an old one — firmly established, popularly supported, and so on. Thus it would seem that the distinction between new prince and old prince isn't at all that important after all; a shrewd new prince can become an instant old prince. And I suppose this is one of the political processes that language can best help with, in the first place by maintaining all the old formulas and routines and associations, and then by infusing the new prince with all the traditional values to which people have got used to responding. Some of this I can do myself by scowling at traditional enemies and smiling benevolently at traditional friends, by flags, emblems, colors, gestures. But getting people to invest these feelings which are tapped by abstract principles in some particular person — getting them to identify a man like me, whom they've never met and hardly seen, with ideas of freedom and justice and so forth and so on — that's a transfer that only language can incite. As a matter of fact, there's very little I can do about it myself; it has to be done for me by a chorus of admiring courtiers whose only reward is likely to be the accusation of flattery. But conscious hypocrisy is out of the question; courtiers understand, from the day they enter the trade, obsequiousness in the hortatory mood. They tell me, and I understand them to be telling me, that I'm a certain sort of chap. And it's this interweaving of what's privately understood with what's publicly stated that constitutes the peculiar advantage of opinion manipulation in a government context. We could perfectly well call it "complicity." But the whole point, as you've doubtless observed, is that in this area I'm using language as a tool to control and manipulate other men. I'm not taking guidance myself, from your little book of formulas, or Egidio Colonna, or Uncle Giovanni, or anyone else. Most of the problems involved in language disappear the minute you are no longer seeking guidance of it, but using it to guide (or misguide) other people. So who, in the end, guides me? Ah, Niccolò, I wish, God knows I wish, there were a formula to follow. There isn't. There can't be. Whoever deludes himself with the thought that because there ought to be, therefore there is, simply hypnotizes himself. No formula, no guide, no crutch.

There is a kind of balance inherent in the situation as we know it.

The word-intoxicated man, the man whose life is built on word manipulation, is obviously going to keep trying to make the formulas subtler
and subtler. Princes who have a little experience with the practical art of
government will know how to discount the word-man: it's a communi-
cations-gap that will be good for everybody. But, oh, Niccoló, Lord save
us all from the day when this little book of yours (and a thousand others
that it will engender) is put in the hands of common folk. If ever that day
comes, when everybody thinks he has a capsule formula of good government, and nobody has any experience to test it against, the whole
enterprise of governing will be next to impossible. The gift you've given
me is a terrible gift; if I thought it would do any good, I'd burn your
manuscript in the palace fireplace. But you authors are all the same —
you would scarcely have sent me this elegant little book if you didn't
have a Xerox® copy stored away somewhere. For all I know, you'll be
smuggling it to a printer one of these days, and then the cat *will* be out
of the bag. The one comfort I take from the whole situation is that people
are stupid enough so they won't realize the extent to which you've
flattered and beguiled them — flattered them in the very simplicity and
clarity of your formulations, with the elegant wit and colloquialism of
your style. I concede that we're all actors in this drama of government,
but what's the point of bringing rank amateurs on stage, and asking
them to improvise believable lines with the help of a playmaker's
formula? The best I can hope for is that they won't understand your
invitation — will be put off by the impression that your little book is
trying to arm *me* against *them*, instead of the contrary. Well, let their
obloquy be your reward. But really, in future, I wish you'd confine your
talents to avowed comedy. You have, I'm persuaded, quite a knack for
it. And you'd be a lot better occupied with that, than in devising cat's
cradles for political leaders to unravel, when they've just been given a
brace of splendid greyhounds to follow, or a spirited Arabian horse to
train. Believe me, Niccoló, I have only your interests at heart. Your book
of rules will tell you how much of that speech to believe.

Yours, &c.
The Magnificent Lorenzo, Duke of Urbino, &c.

*Stultitia to her old friend Desiderius Erasmus*

15 August 1535

Don't be startled, dear boy. I'm not so foolish that I don't understand the sort of welcome a girl is likely to get when she turns up
unexpectedly on the doorstep of an old flame who just happens to be
involved with someone else. Well, you can relax. I haven't the slightest
interest in disturbing your present arrangement with Mistress Prudence.
Our flirtation, if you can call it that, began and ended a full twenty years
ago, and neither of us, as I understand it, has lacked for company since.
Besides, if you'll pardon the indelicacy, you're getting along in years. I
like to think I caught you at just about the last pluckable moment. Now
after a double decade with Mistress Prudence (and I'd be surprised if it
didn't feel like a lot longer than that), you're no fit playmate for the likes
of me. Naturally, I can't take any credit for the way my face and figure
have held up; my mother was Youth herself, and any girl with that
heritage ought to keep her looks, whatever they were to begin with. But
you've been worrying and working — like a fool, I suppose I should say,
since it seems to have paid off chiefly in round shoulders, weak eyes, and
skinny fingers. Only none of my *real* fools would ever be so foolish.

The book we wrote together has been doing very well, I'm told;
that's nice, of course, particularly for you, as a literary man with a
reputation to get and keep. That being the case, I don't suppose I should
mind the story you prefixed to it — really a rather insulting story, if I
were the sort of girl who insulted easily. I mean of course that business
about how you picked me up when you were on a horseback ride from
somewhere to somewhere, played with me en route, and wrote down
my prattle while you were resting and recovering from your trip: saddle-
sores, I daresay. Apart from not being very *galant*, this story rather
strikingly ignores my point of view, don't you think? What do you
suppose I would tell the world if I were to do the telling? "Oh, I was just
hookering along the roadside when a scholar-fellow came by and picked

me up. He put some plapper into my mouth that I didn't understand, and threw me out when I'd served his turn. . . ." Don't you believe it, my fine-feathered scholar; I picked you for my purpose, just as surely as you picked me for yours. And let me ask you just one thing: of all the books you've written before or since, did any ever turn out as well as the one we wrote together? Of course not, you can't deny it. Whereas there are, or will be, any number of writer-fellows who the instant they come across me, suddenly seemed to be a good deal brighter and more entertaining than they were before. You might as well face it: I'm not only witty myself, I'm the cause of wit in others. Of whom — I say it without bragging — you are just one.

This isn't just a personal matter: in fact, it's the reverse of personal. What I'm trying to get at is the fullness of a relation that you've obscured and distorted by writing about it only from your personal point of view. When you describe yourself as indulging momentarily in folly, you carefully give everyone to understand that wisdom was in safe control. It's wise to be foolish now and then; you've even got a little tag of Horatian verse to justify yourself, *dulce est desipere in loco*. And so you account for our escapade, always with the implication that you kept folly on her leash and sent her back to her kennel when fun-time was over. Is it beyond the reach of your imagination to see that folly may have had ends of her own in the association, to fulfil which she made use of wisdom as a momentary and not altogether satisfactory agent? You're used to paradoxes, eh, but that's too much? Let me explain it, then. No, I don't need your doctor's robe, and you needn't put on the dunce's cap, unless association with Madam Prudence has slowed down your wits more than I think.

Look now at the human enterprise on this earth, rooted as it is in instincts and tropisms and appetites and phobias that long antedate any form of wisdom. If, as somebody says, ontogeny recapitulates phylogeny, then every human being should recall from his own experience the squalling, selfish, incontinent bundle of raw appetites which is the first given state of human clay. Culture domesticates these instincts, wisdom partly tempers them, and carves the garden of conscious mind from the jungle luxuriance of instincts. But whatever wisdom mankind possesses or acquires lies cradled in the arms of another and deeper life, with its own imperatives and taboos, a life animated by largely blind instincts toward wholly unknown goals. Have I made my point that wisdom is a mere oarless skiff carried on the strong current of folly? My poor wise

Desiderius, who do you suppose planned the odd circumstances of your birth, or arranged the raggle-taggle Europe in which you've had to live? Has wisdom or folly had a greater share in shaping this history of which man can never hope to stand clear? Obviously, it's the blind animal routine of birth, nutrition, defecation, copulation, and death — the everyday intuitive business of life — that creates human history's current. Let's call this common human heritage natural folly, as opposed to the artificial folly of pedants and philosophers, who pretend to be independent of it. It's the green folly of life's energy, as against the grey folly of abstract and official formulation.

When people are foolishly wise, it's with grey folly; when they are wisely foolish, it's with green. What they are when they use the two forms of folly skeptically, ironically, to complement and correct one another, I shouldn't want to say for fear of falling out of character. But thhis I will say, and can illustrate it from our story, that green folly, whose particular patron I take myself to be, is not only used by, but makes reciprocal use of wisdom for her special ends.

Who doesn't know how hard it is to foresee the future? Beyond our doorstep, over the threshold of tomorrow, lie a thousand chances for disaster, a thousand dangers and challenges and cumulative difficulties before which reason can do nothing but shudder. Who would ever beget a child, found a state, or undertake a social cause if he calculated with cold realism the chances of carrying off each of these enterprises successfully? Fortunately, that's not the spirit in which they are usually approached. Formal wisdom, whose other name is grey folly, is so aware of the perils in life (which is just one tomorrow after another) that her best advice is to sit quietly in a closed room reading a good book about sitting in a closed room reading a good book. Her ideal is contemplative, monastic, stagnant; she thinks, and probably correctly, that the best way to avoid life's problems is to live as little as possible. But green folly thinks it's the height of folly to dwell so long on life's problems that life itself slips away between a wince and a whimper.

It's my lusty green fools who thrust forward into tomorrow, trying new and unproven ideas, clearing the way for developments the consequences of which they don't even want to foresee. They're gamblers by nature, in the service of nature — who would deny it? No wonder my friend Fortune, who you say is always neglecting the wise, prefers my fresh and verdant fools; at least they put some ardor into the petition for her favors. But they aren't just diverting themselves; it's a sacred, saving blindness they undergo, which lets them push forward in the service of the greater life itself, forward into the invisible, dangerous future. Wastrels and chance-takers, the grey fools call them: ridiculous! If they didn't adventure into fresh fields, the wise would sit around chewing the cud of old ideas, long after all the juice had gone out of them. And as I recall, looking back on our friendship, I think it was the sense that you weren't half as wise as you looked that first attracted me to you.

For any man who really relishes deep play with words (as those you call sophists do) appreciates most their power to destroy — they're most fun when they're undercutting one another or their ostensible topic, generating amazement that the wielder doesn't slash himself to bits. Like a sword-dancer, a word-dancer clears an open space around him, within which he seems to live a charmed life — it's a perfectly standard vaudeville routine. Oh, don't you think I wasn't aware of who shared that platform with me, absolutely usurping it toward the end of the performance. You humanists, with your Greek tags and your rhetorical flowers, have never won much acclaim for modesty. I wouldn't presume to describe as folly your obvious delight in your own cleverness (so obvious my dear Erasmus, that you can't write a letter to a friend without making a composition out of it); but I do know it provided an easy handle for me to use in adapting you to my purposes.

What purposes? Why simply to further the disintegration of some restrictive institutions that have, in fact been disintegrating pretty radically since the day of our collaboration. We were out to release — perhaps to provoke, if that were needed — the powers of private judgement. Had you foreseen, Mister Wise Man, all the consequences of our corrosive critical ironies — the hideous controversies, religious wars, burnings and torturings, excommunications and expropriations beyond number — you might have wondered if it was worthwhile to loose that clever critical spirit of yours on the world. All very well for you to glitter as social critic, after the fashion of a scholar and wit; but you didn't foresee, did you, that Luther would criticize like a wild boar and King Henry like a hungry lion. Thus Folly held you in the palm of her hand; and you never thought, never dreamed, of consequences that you find hideous, and only green folly (with her unlimited appetite for fresh life at the expense of disorder) finds desirable or even bearable. It's clear, my friend, she — I — used you and your wisdom in ways which simply helped you dupe yourself with your own cleverness.

I think maybe you suspected something of the sort; for even at the time I noticed certain hedgings and drawings-back, equivocations about even the act of equivocating, which suggested to me that the love of your life was really Madam Prudence. You were always a bit of a flincher, my friend — I speak without offense, of course. If you ask me, it's that agile, disembodied cleverness of yours, that's always pretending to be above or outside any actual situation. It was one of the things I found most trying about our association: any time we were together, there were three of us there, you, me, and that detached wit of yours. I daresay Mistress Prudence has learned to appreciate it — I'm just Folly, and I find myself from time to time in situations where a well-turned epigram simply isn't called for. Probably people felt the same way when you prepared their thoughts for reformation, and then gave them more epigrams on the subject of reformation.

Your friend More, who died so gallantly just last month, wasn't one of my favorite people at all. His death was a piece of folly of course, but grey folly, not green. Still, I'm not so confined to my allegory that I can't recognize the presence of supreme grace — I use the word in its human sense, but if anyone wants to find another, that's all right for me. What I mean is that undivided sense of whole-hearted being that comes when a man goes beyond formulas, as can be done every so often, even in the act of affirming them. Folly and wisdom may walk hand in hand, then, perhaps in combination with some force that philosophy herself would be hard put to divine. And then again there's something called cleverness that spends its time devising verbal formulas to avoid — if you'll excuse my saying so — putting its ass on the ground in any particular place. It's a funny thing when you think of it, that the brightest and wisest are so often also the meanest of mankind. But that's a fool's wisdom. You'll figure out, with the help of Mistress Prudence, another way to look at things.

Farewell,

Folly

*Ippolito Cardinal d'Este to Lodovico Ariosto*

March, 1520

My dear Messer Lodovico,

Ugh! I've just returned from one of those formal dinners at the palace of Cardinal Bakocz, complete with spicy goulash and heavy sweet wines which I'm sure you recall only too vividly. Who was the ghastly joker who named the late king of this country after a raven? — though, as I recall, his actual character was more like that of a sparrow. Lord knows I've tried, by irony and innuendo and indirection (everything short of open rudeness) to make clear that the Italian stomach, the Italian liver, are used to lighter fare. No use. The only concession they'll make for us foreigners is to throw more coals in the stoves — as if the rooms weren't suffocatingly hot already. So when the evening is over, stuffed and sweaty and rolled up in furs, we're bundled out into our coaches for the frosty ride home. What a way to live!

Believe me, as we make our way home through the dark and the cold, we often think of you at Ferrara with your modest circumstances — your small home with a servant or two, your rented horse, your modest diet, your aged mother, your several children and *their* several mothers, your elegant Horatian verses. Oh yes, word of those unsatiric little satires has penetrated even to us here at Buda, or is it Pesth? And we find it comforting to know that somewhere at least the light, civilized touch is still being cultivated. Has anybody thought to compare your satires with a glass of cold Frascati? I won't push the analogy any further than to say that it's my absolute favorite wine, combining briskness on the outside with a quiet glow on the inside, providing discourse as richly humane as is possible in any other medium.

Our parting, as I recall, wasn't without bitterness on both sides, and there's no pretending that an ugly word doesn't sometimes crop up among the retinue here when your name is mentioned. It's the old feudal spirit at work, of course — a kind of surly, righteous feeling that when a retainer has eaten a prince's bread for years, accepting of his largesse and ease such as it may be, it simply isn't honorable to slink off when the service becomes disagreeable. Mind you, I'm not endorsing this language or even this idea, which seems to me ridiculously old-fashioned, as doubtless it does to you. But that's the way people talk. I've tried to smooth matters over — not very effectively, I fear. What bothers me most, I think, is what some of them call the "tradesman's" spirit at the end of your second satire, in which you offer to give back the rewards you've received, in return for release from onerous obligation. A fine thing, say they — as if Orlando were to surrender his dukedom and give up his honors, in order to get out of a dangerous battle with Rodomonte or Agramante.

You see what ridiculous lengths they go to, these grumblers. I've told them they're being absurd. Messer Lodovico, I said, isn't a medieval paladin; he's a modern poet. He has a gift beyond the rest of us, apart from our vulgar, utilitarian talents. If we're remembered at all, with our petty pride and petty service and petty politics, it will be because of his poem. When he sits in a room at Ferrara, all by himself, composing verses, that's a service of a higher sort than fifty embassies to Hungary or two hundred legations to Julius II. For he is representing us to posterity — so I say — and posterity isn't fifty men or two hundred, it's an infinitude. As long as Italian is read, Messer Lodovico will be our window to immortality: we should be grateful to him for mentioning us, even if he does so only to call us ingrates.

I haven't made much headway with this line of argument, but, given time and patience, perhaps I will.

The real trouble, Messer Lodovico, lies in your talent, your poetry, your poem. In every respect, our relations are simple and clear, as they are with all my other servants and courtiers; only in your case, I must divide my jurisdiction with the Muses. I'm not jealous of those ladies, not in the least; for all I know, you've used service to my brother or me as an excuse for resisting some command of theirs. What's perfectly certain is that you've used service to them as an excuse for resisting commands of mine. Dual citizenship of this sort must be a thoroughly agreeable arrangement; I only wish I could arrange some if it for myself.

For of course I've not been able to resign, decline, or refuse any sort of responsibility since the day Duke Ercole decided that, as his third son, I must be given a career in the church. You no doubt recall, but I'll remind you anyway, that I was just five years old when he made me an abbot of Canalnovo (a commendatory abbot, but only five years old!), seven when I picked up this accursed Hungarian connection by becoming archbishop of Esztergom, and fourteen when the hat descended — as if by magic, from nowhere, in the hands of Alexander VI. Later on, it turns out that all these nice offices mean you have to wear out your life in Hungary. Being third son of the House of Este means you have to fight tooth and nail, an eye for an eye, so to speak, against your own blood-kin — well, there's no use laboring that point. I was pushed at my birth into a set of positions, each with its good points and its bad ones, long before I had anything to say about "accepting" or "declining" the office; and now, even if I wanted to, do you suppose I could follow something as simple as my pleasure, as gratifying as my "talent"? Never, never. Apart from the gossip of Ferrara, do you realize, Lodovico, what my Italian mail mostly consists of? Letters from my builders at Tivoli, who are putting up a villa there for our family. Don't you suppose I'd rather be there, drinking Frascati, dawdling among the Roman matrons, and supervising the Roman masons, than here, eating strudel and goulash among the barbarians? I think, in fact, I have a sort of gift for architectural fantasy; it torments me, sometimes, to think what a wild and wonderful villa I could put up, if I could only be in Rome to do it. Well, I can't, so this sort of daydreaming is out of the question. I'm the prisoner of my birth; but you, by being reborn in words as a poet of the highest rank, have acquired a whole new set of freedoms — not just one more world, but your choice of worlds for different occasions. I confess to a distinct sense of envy.

I've been meaning to ask how the big poem, the "Orlando," is being received — not that I have any real doubts of its enormous success. Apart from all the loyal friends whom you arranged to have present in Canto 46 as a welcoming committee, the poem is bound to make its way even with foreign readers, strangers to us all, by virtue of a kind of gaiety and playfulness which in literature at least has no visible drawbacks. Oh, in a serious way I'm bound no doubt to express my gratitude, and that of my illustrious house, for your celebration of Ruggiero, whose nuptials with Bradamante gave rise to what's-his-name, who begat, who begat, and so all the way down the long genealogy to, I suppose, Alphonso and me. Well, it's nice to be reminded that the family tree has roots among Charlemagne's paladins, though one does sound rather stuffy raising the topic in a casual social context. The point needs no emphasis for a man of your tact; indeed, the poem itself comes close to making it. You may think me ungenerous, but I got the distinct sense from riffling through the story that Ruggiero was less than passionately interested in Bradamante in the first place. Why else was he constantly seeking trivial excuses for going off on long and dangerous expeditions? And of course she had no interest at all in him as a person; like all women, she was more impressed by genealogy than personality, and if Merlin hadn't filled her with romantic nonsense about the glorious destiny awaiting her off-spring by Ruggiero, I doubt if she'd have turned her head to look at the paladin in the street. And then all the long ceremonial folderol about their marriage! Perhaps I'm altogether wrong in my literary judgements, but it struck me that Astolfo and Angelica were characters to whom you gave a great deal more of your literary sympathy. And I think I see why, too. They're elusive, evasive, fantastic characters; they live, like you, in two worlds at once, and manage to get the best of both of them.

Angelica is the worst. What were you thinking of, Messer Lodovico, when you changed her so from Messer Boiardo's perfectly honorable (if slightly wooden) heroine? Why, there's not a single heroic thing she does in the whole poem — unless you consider it heroic in a girl to fascinate Orlando, the great Orlando, out of his wits, and then slither off with a silly little pagan boy — on the pretext, forsooth, that she was in love with him. Why *should* she be in love with him? He hadn't won any battles, hadn't performed any particular service, wasn't deserving on any score. Yet you have the Princess of Circassia fall in love with him (not he with her, you make that pretty clear, but she with him), and off they go in the middle of the poem, to a world of pastoral bliss, to Circassia, to the devil knows where. It's as if she were snubbing, not only the other characters, and the whole social system, but your own poem. . . . I know, you say you disapprove, you criticize her and her cruelty to Orlando; but it's per-fectly apparent that your real opinion is exactly the contrary. That's another consequence of you literary people living in two worlds at once: you're always saying one thing, and meaning it maybe, but meaning something else too, which is contradictory, or seems so to us readers who try to live only in one world at a time.

There was a passage in the poem that particularly struck me, where Orlando, seeking Angelica in his madness, captures her mare instead. I think it's at the end of Canto 29. He gallops off on the beast — naked, hairy, muscular, mindless Orlando —, rides it to death, and then struggles on, carrying the dead horse on his shoulders or dragging it behind him.

What a picture of passion! It's surely your masterpiece as a scene. It's ludicrous, it's horrifying, it's pathetic, all at once. You say, of course, that the whole thing was Angelica's fault, even that it would have served her right if Orlando had caught her instead of the mare, and treated her in the same way. Obviously you don't mean that, you can't. Your readers will be horrified at the very thought, and you know they will; you've overstated deliberately, to produce a reaction in Angelica's favor. Orlando's entire madness, which is the theme of your poem, would become repellent and disgusting if it led him to butcher a lady like Angelica, who's more delicate and delightful than he — and there you go again. You've made Angelica, who's an irresponsible, self-centered bitch (I'm sorry, but it's the best name I can give her), far more attractive than the serious, responsible Orlando. What you want is for Angelica to get off morally scot-free, leaving the rewards and punishments all out of balance. Late in the poem, Rinaldo for no particular reason sets off to take vengeance on Angelica, but he encounters the monster Jealousy, from whom he is rescued by Disdain — and that's the end of redressing the moral balance. What you're reproducing in Rinaldo, I suppose, is the reaction of the reader, who recognizes that he's jealous of Medoro, and so turns back from any sort of moral judgement of Angelica. But that leaves Orlando and his grievance and the whole question of "service" in love, altogether up in the air. Besides, Rinaldo can't disdain her, because she's already disdained him, and everything he stands for. As for poor Orlando, it's because he's so serious and responsible (wouldn't you say?) that he goes crazy when faced with a wayward witch like Angelica. And yet your sympathies, if you have any real ones, are with her. Or so it seemed to me.

If Angelica causes Orlando to lose his wits, Astolfo is the means by which he recovers them. To be perfectly frank, neither one of them is a serious personage. Astolfo isn't a responsible warrior, he's a player of games who flitters around the edges of things. His flight to the moon is a flight of fancy — isn't that what you're saying? And yet it's this airy, hare-brained British lunatic who brings Orlando's wits back from the moon, and stuffs them up his nose like a pinch of snuff. You doubtless appreciate that this arrangement of forces makes a farce of the heroic narrative. A hero whose wits can be adjusted, as it were, with a twist of the wrist and a sniff at the bottle, isn't a hero any more, he's a gadget. I'm not telling you anything here you don't already know. A hero for you poets is just a name to which a lot of stories can be attached. When you've used up the serious stories, you tell silly ones. And that's fine for your poem. Its readers won't be heroes, any more than you're a hero yourself. They'll enjoy heroic adventures (as recited in your civilized, semi-serious verses), and they'll also enjoy feeling superior to them. So you have your subject and you have your stance against the subject — one again, both ways.

As I've set up this matter to think about, duplicity figures as a basic literary attitude; but once you get in the way of it, there's apparently no natural stopping point. For I seem to see you, throughout your poem, playing all sorts of half-derisive games with literature itself. What else is the point of all those borrowings from classical fable? Half the time you don't even point them out, just have your characters run through and pick up the connection. I won't even try to make a list, but when Ruggiero astride the hippogriff rescues Angelica from the orc, we're obviously supposed to think of Perseus on Bellerophon rescuing Andromeda from the sea monster. Astolfo liberates Senape (Prester John, right?) from the torment of the harpies, just as Phineas was liberated from the harpies by the Argonauts. The story of Bireno and Olimpia is just like that of Theseus and Ariadne; the story of Norandino and *his* orc parallels that of Ulysses and his companions in the cave of Polyphemus; and the night-raid of Cloridan and Medoro recalls that of Nisus and Euryalus in the "Aeneid" — which, of course, recalls that of Ulysses and Diomede in the "Iliad." These stories of yours aren't parodies, nor yet modernizings, if only because your own story is essentially antique. The main thing that attaches to them is the pleasure of recognition, a joining into the charmed ring of complicity that I venture to say will be thought in future your special and characteristic effect. How you do it, I wont venture to say; but it's a regular trick of yours, as subtle as a smile or a momentary intonation of intimacy. You tell people what they've never dreamed or imagined, but in such a way as to convince them, not only that they've know it all the time, but that knowing it has been a bond of sympathy between them, a mark of distinction. By not questioning what is in fact questionable, they give evidence of being in on a previous secret, a private Ariostean vision. And thus you turn off conflicts and problems, questions of moral or social judgement, not vulgarly, God knows, with a nudge and a leer, but between a smile and an evasion — "Well, what did you expect?" That question isn't far from a put down.

Homer and Virgil and our own Dante are architects in literature; the structures they put up stand foursquare at a distance to be measured and admired. Your work is more like a conversation between yourself and a circle of friends; it's intimate, animated, fluent, and each member of the circle carries away from it a different impression of what you said. No doubt you know what you're doing; but it's my impression that people who are serious about the literary structure of values will feel that you diminish it, as do people who are serious about social values. Why should you care? I don't suppose you should or will. Your reward will lie in the acclaim of a few happy souls, attuned to your own, who won't want to analyze or measure or define your poem, but who will take it as a piece of overheard and shared conversation. For the privilege of living in that enchanted landscape, they won't care whom or what they abandon. Or rather, the more they abandon, and the more carelessly (*naturally!*) they do so, the more forcefully they demonstrate themselves your true adepts, sharers of the special vision.

In this way you liberate language as it liberates you, not to a larger or deeper sense of this world, but to another world altogether. While I read your poem, I feel I know Messer Lodovico as a wholly different person from the man of flesh and blood who served our family through all the thick and some of the thin for so many years. He is a living, growing book, and perhaps all the better for it. Being a book, he is in some sense all books; language is growing inside him like a peach tree or perhaps like a mushroom-patch, and using all the books ever written to fulfill itself. That makes you sound rather like your chosen hero, doesn't it? Like most plants grown in a special environment (one perhaps deliberately created to foster certain qualities), there's something strange as well as wonderful, something closely akin to madness, about poetry of this order. It seems to be the creation of a second nature, or of a kind of folding-back on its own nature, so that the poem becomes its own environment, and opens the way for infinite recessions. Word-grown personalities, deliberately forced in verbal hothouses, creating an atmosphere in which still other and more exotic blooms will flourish — doubtless this is a pattern for the future. As a person with most of his roots in the old nature, the plain and common one, I don't regard the development with much enthusiasm. (You yourself may be aware of owing a good deal to our social Italian love of conversation, which keeps at least one of your feet on the ground most of the time.) But who's the Astolfo who's going to restore their wits to the poets of the future when they start down your path? I couldn't afford more than one Ariosto in my court; and if your successor is a mad as Orlando — which I rather anticipate — *my* successor won't be able to afford even one.

Between us, we seem to have developed the making of a first-rate impasse. It will be interesting to see how, in the long run, it develops. Or doesn't develop.

My compliments to all our friends in Ferrara, from their friend in exile,


Ippolito, Cardinal d'Este

◆

# III. CANTO NINE

major poet of the Italian renaissance was interrupted in the composition of his supreme epic accomplishment when his country was invaded by alien enemy armies. He plunged into the fighting and died within three months, leaving his poem incomplete and at a curiously interesting stage of the action. What we can tell about its possible future development is naturally a matter of speculation. But from the shape being taken by the final incomplete canto, as well as from the character of the 77 cantos already written, and the direction taken by the poet's previous life, our surmises can be more or less guided into more or less informed channels. That is the aim of this paper. Part one deals with the poet's life and published work, part two is a translation of the last fragmentary canto of his poem, and part three is a close speculation about the immediate direction the poem might have taken, had the poet been spared for a few more cantos.

Matteo Maria Boiardo, count of Scandiano, lived in the second half of the 15th century (1434-1494), and grew up on the several estates of his family in the neighborhood of Reggio nell' Emilia. He must have studied the principles of jurisprudence at the university at Ferrara, for most of his life was passed as an official of the government of the dukes of Este, who commanded Ferrara and the neighboring districts. Boiardo's business letters, of which many survive, are severely dry and businesslike; at his death he was military governor of Reggio. But on the side, for whatever combination of prudential and artistic motives, he cultivated the muses.

The muse of history in the first place. Cornelius Nepos wrote some lives of distinguished men, and Boiardo or one of his secretaries translated some of them, as well as the *Cyropedia* of Xenophon and the *Golden Ass* of Apuleius. Apparently the young lord touched up, at the last minute, the heavy work done by his subordinates on these projects. On his own he wrote a little group of Latin eclogues, another group of "vulgar" or Italian poems, and for a social occasion he compounded a single Lucianic comedy on the subject of "Timon." The exact dates of these "minor works" are nor known with any accuracy, and none of them seem to have been published very close to the time when they were written. Then in the two years 1469-1471 the poet undertook two extended and very diverse projects on which his reputation now largely rests. One was a collection of lyrics in three books, known either as *Amorum Libri* or *Il Canzioniere*. The alternate titles suggest alternate derivations from Ovid and Petrarch, and while both intimations are accurate, both influences were largely modified by acquaintance with other Italian amorists, not excluding Boccaccio. Because of the plethora of predecessors and competitors in this field, it is hard to pronounce on the merits of the *Amorum Libri*, which has been praised to the skies and dismissed with condescension. But from the first it was overshadowed in popularity by Boiardo's other major achievement, the epic *Orlando Innamorato*. Both appeared at very much the same time, with the implication that they must have been composed almost simultaneously. This is remarkable in that the two works are radically diverse in theme, structure, and vocabulary. It would not be hard to conclude that they were the work of two entirely different poets. But the *Orlando*, begun at the same time as the *Amorum Libri* continued to grow, as it was intended to do, to epic proportions.

Poems about Orlando, or Roland as he is known in French and English, were far from an absolute novelty when Boiardo took up the subject. They were a major element in the collection of myths know as *chansons de geste*; they had been given a semi-serious turn by Pulci in his comic epic *Morgante*. Having Orlando, the paladin of Charlemagne, fall in love was a conscious novelty on Boiardo's part. Love, as he deliberately explains, had been the traditional province of the matter of Brittany, the stories of King Arthur and his court. In the same measure that Roland, Oliver, and the others are in service to Charlemagne, so Lancelot, Tristram, and the knights of the Round Table are in service to their ladies. But Boiardo's title promises a mixture of both these themes, and actually provides it, with a great deal more. The encompassing theme of the epic is the aggressive war waged by Gradasso, king of Sericana, against Charlemagne, ruler of France and leader of western Europe. Among the tangible prizes of this conflict will be the sword Durindana and the steed Baiardo, but really it is the government of Charlemagne, his sovereignty over the west, that is at stake. Armies, kings, barons, and paladins are lined up to defend the emperor; the attacking armies are just as immense and varied. But the solidarity of both armies is shattered by the appearance in their midst of Angelica, daughter of King Galifrone of Cathay. She is a pagan and the daughter of a pagan; she is accompanied by four sinister giants, protected by a magic ring which renders her invisible, and surrounded by an aura of magic which ought to give Orlando pause. In all sorts of ways she is different from the Nice Christian Girl who would be a proper companion for our hero; but she is so fascinatingly lovely that he falls wildly in love with her, as does the entire baronage and most of the pagan assemblies as well. Thus we are embarked on a long and tangled story in which Orlando and Angelica often drop from sight for long periods of time while other warriors and damsels carry on subordinate intrigues, while armies shift from continent to continent, while magic swords clash on magic armor, while tourneys are organized and fought to keep the warriors occupied.

For if there is one activity to which all Boiardo's people are partial, it is fighting — organized warfare if it happens to be going on, individual duels or group melées if that's the form it takes. There is no spirit of lighthearted play; the fighting is deadly serious. The heros smash each other over the head, they take mighty two-handed swipes with their swords which cut the opponent vividly in two, they plunge unhesitatingly into free-for-alls from which heads, arms, and torsos fly out as from a mechanical meat-chopper. The historic model for the biggest battles seems to be that fought out between the eastern forces of Attila and those of the west under Aetius. This is half a millennium or so out of the age of Charlemagne, since Chalons was fought in 451; besides, it did not involve Moors from Africa but Huns from the remote Orient; still, Boiardo makes so little pretense of historical accuracy that details like this hardly matter. His Moors swear by and sometimes pray to Macone or Macon or Macometto; he does not seem to know of Allah or the Koran, of mosques, imams, or particular religious observances. Moors are exotic because of their elaborate names which there is reason to think Boiardo elaborated from the more peculiar names or nicknames of peasants on his properties. But there is no generic difference of creed or comportment between the warriors of the opposing armies. All paladins are paladins together — much admired and much feared, but with little specific motivation, apart from belligerence for its own sake. The Christians in particular are totally innocent about accepting the woeful tale of any damsel declaring herself to be in distress. This is specially foolish because enchantments are so many and misleading, and damsels so deceitful, that one would think the knights ought to be just the least mistrustful. But the heroes' faults of judgement are almost always redeemed by their feats of derring-do. Quite a number of Christian heroes are defeated at one point by a specially guileful enemy who stashes them in the bottom of a lake. But no need to worry, they survive cheerfully there and are rescued in due course by a fellow-paladin.

Thus the epic proceeds on its own course, accumulating characters and episodes freely and unhurriedly. After two books of 29 and 31 cantos each, it has not even come within sight of the siege of Paris which is supposed to be the central action of the poem. (But this is not a rock-solid proposition.) Stylistically, it is a mixed bag, sometimes rough and jocose, sometimes lyrical and exalted, bluff and hearty at some moments and at others immediately conversational. Boiardo had composed about one third of book 3 (assuming it was to be on the scale of books 1 and 2) when the work was cut short by the unexpected invasion of Italy by French troops under Charles VIII. At 60, the poet was beyond the age of active military duty, but as military governor of Reggio many of the administrative problems of the invasion and resistance fell on his shoulders and he did not support them long.

His poem had from the beginning a frivolous and a serious component; it was playful, fantastic, and entertaining, and it also asserted vigorously the antiquity and authority of the ruling house of Este. The dynasty was far from well established in the city of Ferrara; it needed, or thought that it needed, a founding mythology, and that Boiardo undertook to provide. Apart from that, his compositional procedures were, to say the least, distinctive. He composed the poem, a canto at a time, alone by himself, while wandering across the open fields of his ancestral acres. His next step was to bring the finished canto to court, where he would recite it to an invited audience, accompanying his verses on the same lyre or harp to which they had originally been written. Having an audience to entertain, he used the common tricks of the serial story-teller, breaking off an action *in medias res*, tantalizing his hearers with a promise of juicy episodes to come, and so on. At the court of Duke Ercole he rejoiced in an audience of great urbanity and quick wit — one of the most sophis-ticated, surely, in Europe. Its social values were not only aristocratic but after a fashion medieval, such as remind one from time to time of certain frescoes of Pisanello and of his drawings. By Boiardo's day there were in real life few or no paladins; chivalry, if not dead, was moribund. One of its destroyers was actually present in the court that Boiardo amused, in the person of Ercole's successor Alfonso, soon to be third duke of Este. He was in his day the greatest artilleryman in Europe; and nobody did more to destroy not only the knights and knight-errantry but the armor and fortifications that made knights effective warriors. Nostalgia thus overlies Boiardo's poem as tangibly as it does Pisanello's paintings, but with an edge of humor and occasionally a touch of mordant realism, as of a man who will not gladly be his own fool.

Substantially, this is the note on which the *Orlando Innamorato* concludes, or at least comes to a stop. Orlando does not ever get close to Angelica; Agramante and his Moorish peers have no chance whatever of dethroning Charlemagne or capturing Paris; Rinaldo de Montalbano wanders off into his own labyrinthine story, which will take many romantic narratives to complete. Boiardo's poem ends in the middle of the preliminaries leading up (perhaps) to the siege of Paris. In the course of these struggles, Bradamante, who is the daughter of Amon of Chiarmont (Clermont) and thus the sister of Rinaldo and his three brothers, has been particularly active in fighting Daniforte of Tunis, an unusually despicable Saracen whom, in a desperate hand-to-hand encounter, she kills. But she is badly wounded, wanders away from the fields of battle, and takes refuge in the hut of a nearby hermit. He heals her wounds, cutting off her hair in the process, but is appalled to discover that she is a woman. Fearful lest she be a presentation of the devil, he drives her away; and Bradamante, thus outcast, wanders off to lie down in a quiet grove by a brook. Sleeping peacefully here, she is discovered by Fiordespina, daughter of Marsillo, king of Spain, who just happens to have wandered into these deep woods, totally oblivious of the tremendous battle going on nearby. Fiordespina is accompanied by a band of private retainers; her mission is simply to hunt some deer. She neither knows nor cares about the siege of Paris, or anything else that has happened in the narrative so far.

These ladies or women trailing in or around a major battle are a frequent though not clearly explained feature of the poem's scenario. Both Firdelisa and Fiordespina have taken intermittent brief parts in the poem's action since the early cantos. Bradamante is of a very valiant and noble family, though she does not do as much fighting, for example, as Marfisa. But Fiordelisa is a bit of a camp follower who, when she earlier took up with Brandimarte, a very noble and courteous Saracen, did not hesitate to let nature take its course in a shady grove of the forest. Six times without a pause the happy couple tied the knot (book 1, canto 19) before their ardor diminished, and the war could proceed. The poet offers no comment on their doings, which have no matrimonial intent or consequence. The episode is an episode of the war, and the same might be said about the encounter of Fiordespina with Bradamante, except that Bradamante seems to be a person of unusual consequence. But neither lady is central to the war — if, indeed, the war is central to the poem. So how seriously to take the whole episode is a matter for the reader's individual judgement. Meanwhile, we had best turn to Boiardo's poem itself — or more precisely, to the partial ninth canto of the unfinished third book of the *Orlando Innamorato*, which opens with the poet's frank address to his noble auditors.

### 1

*Since, then, my song has brought you such delight,*
*The signs of which are clearly manifest*
*In all your faces, let me lift my flight,*
*Call on my finest lyre, and so request*
*The Lord of Love to lift me to his height*
*So that our voices join, and fill my breast*
*With song; or if too far I do aspire,*
*Let me at least breathe of his sacred fire.*

### 2

*As the sun rising at the break of day*
*While stars still glitter on the dewy lawn,*
*Such is this court in honor's bright array,*
*Ladies and lords under the glowing dawn,*
*On whom, O Love, you shed a glorious ray*
*From which you will not gladly be withdrawn.*
*O rest within this perfect circle, Love.*
*And you'll not ever miss the spheres above.*

3

*For here you'll find another paradise; —*
*But for the present, of your perfect store*
*Breathe wisdom on me that I may suffice,*
*To tell how Fiordespina more and more,*
*Gazing on Bradamante, found her eyes*
*Drawn on that single perfect face to pore,*
*Until the focus of her fiery gaze*
*Melted her self like wax beneath the solar blaze.*

4

*— Nor turned away her steady, avid glance*
*Which grew more eager as it fed more deep,*
*Like moths, which cannot break the candle's trance*
*Till quite consumed. Like widely scattered sheep,*
*The huntsmen with their dogs — all whines and pants —*
*Lounged on the grass, one raucous tangled heap*
*Of hawks, dogs, horses, men and tack,*
*The noise of which caused Amon's daughter to wake.*

5

*From eyes that open suddenly*
*There springs a light, a sudden blaze*
*That shines on Fiordespina specially,*
*And sinks at once into her bosom's maze,*
*Reflecting back for anyone to see*
*What her face all too vividly displays,*
*That rosy blush which in the early morn*
*Tells nature that it's time to be reborn.*

6

*And Bradamante had by now arisen,*
*And, knowing well by traits of gait and guise*
*That this must be some dame of rich bedizen*
*And lofty status, tried herself to rise*
*And to recall her own present position,*
*Struggling as best she might both to surmise*
*Where now she was, and most particularly where*
*She tethered, just the night before, her mare.*

7

*Having herself knotted the bridle tight*
*Before she went off wandering in the wood,*
*She now felt such a chill, uneasy fright*
*As half suffused her vision in a flood*
*Of crystal tears. But Love, with sure insight,*
*Taught Fiordespina how she could*
*Assist this baffled cavalier, with whom*
*She found herself so suddenly alone.*

8

*A horse she had of Andalusian breed,*
*So light and free of foot that on the track*
*He had no paragon — of peerless speed,*
*And yet one fault he had, or rather lack:*
*When set in motion, this unruly steed*
*Could never stop, whoe'er was on his back,*
*Except at certain words — a secret sealed*
*Which his bold mistress never had revealed.*

9

*With this rare beast she hoped to gain the prize*
*Of Bradamante's self, whom she supposed*
*A man of war; and on this surmise,*
*"Baron," she said, "you seem ill-disposed,*
*And at a loss without your horse; take my advice,*
*And, better yet, the offer I propose,*
*Based solely on your noble features,*
*Which mirror (as they say) the souls of creatures.*

10

*Most often what is good is also fair,*
*And thus I cannot grant to anyone*
*Better than you a gift that I count rare:*
*This horse of mine is, underneath the sun,*
*The fastest, boldest, most courageous mare*
*That any cavalier did ever own.*
*A trifling gift's a trifle to impart,*
*But precious gifts are given from the heart."*

11

*So saying, from the saddle she alit,*
*And with the bridle did the mare present,*
*While Bradamante, who did not omit*
*To note her flushing cheeks and lame accént,*
*Thought to herself, "Now here's a pretty fit,*
*Someone will not be very well content*
*When pretty soon she happens to remark*
*Grater on grater yields no kind of spark."*

12

*So inwardly did Bradamante muse; but then, aloud*
*Spoke to the Lady: "This gift is such that I*
*With all I am and all with which endowed*
*Could never in my lifetime make reply.*
*But compliments are for the vulgar crown*
*To bandy back and forth; you and I*
*Are on another plane, and you may take*
*Whate'er you will of me for your own sake."*

13

*"Before so high a gift I cannot dream*
*Of hesitating," Fiordespina said;" for ne'er before*
*Did such a gift encounter, as I deem,*
*So noble a response." But now the maid of war*
*Moved toward the courser in a silver gleam*
*And at a single bound in full armór*
*Sprang to the saddle — no use of stirrups here,*
*She moved as light as any forest deer.*

14

*The Moorish lady looked upon this feat*
*With widened eyes and ever-watchful gaze,*
*Then, drawing up her entourage complete,*
*Spoke to them thus: "For these present days*
*This hunt has been arranged to my conceit*
*And for my pleasure only. Who disobeys*
*My order now, and falls on my displeasure*
*Will undergo my anger in full measure.*

15

*"I want you all to stay exactly here,*
*Keeping your camp within this quiet vale,*
*And leave unharmed for now the wandering deer;*
*Let them be mine, if so I may prevail*
*But you, oh baron, be you always near,*
*That we may share the pleasures of the trail,*
*Those wildwood pleasures that are quite*
*Of all diversions my supreme delight."*

16

*At once they hasten to obey,*
*Unstring the bows and call the dogs to heel;*
*The noise within the forest dies away,*
*No further sound of trumpet, hoof or wheel,*
*When suddenly a buck in full display*
*Of branching antlers did himself reveal,*
*Bursting from cover so fast that human eye*
*Could scarcely note his figure flashing by.*

17

*Across the open sward he broke so fast*
*No thorn or briar could arrest his course,*
*As quickly as a lightning bolt he passed*
*Within an inch of Fiordespina's horse,*
*Yet stopped short there, as to say, "I may compass*
*This one, and draw her, fearing nothing worse."*
*The lady turned, as if to agree,*
*And to her liege said simply, "Follow me."*

18

*At once she caught the bridle in her hand*
*To chase the deer wherever he might lead,*
*And of her follower made the same demand.*
*Her horse was of the famous Irish breed,*
*Swift as a whippet, like most beasts of that land,*
*Though not like Bradamante's horse for speed —*
*Which gave her owner new occasion to repent*
*Because the pace was faster than she meant.*

19

*Her horse indeed was galloping so fast*
*As left her rider not a breath to cry*
*Or call aloud when she closed in and passed*
*The horse of Fiordespina on the fly,*
*By then the rider was herself aghast,*
*Seeing that howsoever she did try*
*To rein the creature in, the flying beast*
*Paid no attention to her, not the least.*

20

*They paused before a steep and rocky tor*
*Covered with strange and unfamiliar trees;*
*For beasts like theirs this was no sort of bar,*
*They flew across as wafted on a breeze;*
*Beside the deer they rode, or a bit before,*
*While Fiordespina stayed alert to seize*
*The proper path, and keep the hunt together,*
*Bunched as if held upon a single tether.*

21

*As they came bounding down the steep incline,*
*The deer got tangled with a snarling hound;*
*At once the other eager dogs combine*
*To drag their prey, still struggling, to the ground —*
*Which brought her prey to Fiordespina's mind;*
*She could not let him get too far beyond*
*Her reach, so raised the special call*
*She used to bring her horse back to his stall.*

22

*No need to ask did Bradamante find*
*Relief in sudden rest; as quick as sound*
*She slipped out of the saddle, and resigned*
*Herself to standing on the common ground,*
*Her heart still beating fast having behind*
*Her eyes the thought of instant death; now she found*
*The voice of Fiordespina at her ear,*
*With soft apologies and gentle cheer.*

23

*"Twas my omission, not my fault; I do not know*
*How I forgot to tell you one need only say*
*Sharply into his ear the one word, 'Whoa!'*
*That single word he always will obey.*
*But this was my mistake, I know not how,*
*The crucial timely formula to convey —*
*A careless, silly fault, which yet*
*I have not words to say how I regret."*

24

With this plea Bradamante was content,
And even ventured cautiously to ride,
The more so, when by slow experiment
She found the horse would instantly subside,
Just hearing once the magic word; and so they went
More peacefully together, toward a wide
But level lawn, shaded by a ridge;
A little stream ran through it with a bridge.

25

Here now the ladies' hands together grew,
Bradamante still in silver armor cased,
While Fiordespina's gown was midnight blue,
With golden stars and ornaments enlaced;
Both light and lovely as the morning dew,
They might the entire world have graced.
One for the other burned with secret fire,
Save for one single lack, not for my lyre.

26

But, great redeeming God, even while I sing,
I see all Italy burst into flame
From these ferocious Gauls, who come to bring
Rape and destruction, or to proclaim
Who knows what future griefs? This cosmic swing
Now calls me far from my poetic aim
To tell of Fiordespina's love; another time,
If it be granted, must serve for that rhyme.

This is to end the poem with a meat-cleaver, leaving the gash raw and bloody. But why not accept Ariosto's completion of Boiardo's story? In addition to his many other borrowings from the earlier epic, Ariosto undertook in Canto 25 of the *Furioso* to build the story of Fiordespina toward a proper conclusion. According to this continuation, Fiordespina carries off Bradamante to an inn or hostel at a nearby town where she makes the unhappy discovery that her beloved is a female. For the rest of the night, which they spend in a common bed, Fiordespina is restless and tormented, Bradamante calm and indifferent, perhaps simply asleep. (Meanwhile Fiordespina's hunting party, forgotten by everyone, continues to camp in the woods where they have been ordered to stay. Nobody will ever tell them to go home.) But, with the dawn, the ladies must now, however reluctantly, say goodbye. Fiordespina sets off toward her father's kingdom in Spain, while Bradamante returns to her family, now centered on Rinaldo's castle at Montalbano. There she tells her story to, among others, the younger brother of the family, one Ricciardetto. Hitherto he has been a very minor young man whom his big brother Rinaldo feels obliged to protect from mischief, his own as well as others'. But he suddenly turns out, in Ariosto's telling of the story, to resemble Bradamante miraculously. Thus, hearing his sister's romantic tale, he sees a place in it for himself and takes off secretly in pursuit of Fiordespina. He introduces himself, tells the lady a cock-and-bull story about having undergone a magical sex-change, and after suitable concealings backed by very little persuasion, is received into her bed and into her household. Here he remains successfully for a while in the function of a secret gigolo or stud.

This clandestine arrangement can hardly be described as a satisfactory solution to the difficulties of Fiordespina and Bradamante, both of whom have been grossly deceived; it cannot be the sort of dénouement that Boiardo had in mind when he brought the two ladies together. When Fiordespina's father becomes aware of the deception, his reaction (with which a Renaissance audience would doubtless have felt a good deal of sympathy), was to burn Riccardietto at the stake. The young rascal was rescued by the timely intervention of a fellow paladin, but that is hardly to his credit. As for Fiordespina, nothing more is said of her, which doubtless means that she is understood to have disappeared into a formidable nunnery, where she would spend the rest of her wretched years.

There are other problems with Arioso's continuation. Riccardietto (who cannot, in English, be other than Little Richard), when suddenly introduced at the end of Canto Nine to complete the Boiardo story, would have been absent from the poem or over 1,100 pages — his name not even spoken for that period. The most devoted of audiences could hardly have been expected to remember him so long. His resemblance to Bradamante has never been mentioned, let alone emphasized. His behavior is in the highest degree unknightly; in being satisfied with him on the terms proposed (in functional terms, he is nothing but the common masculine appendage), Fiordespina degrades not only herself but her entire relation with Bradamante. Indeed, Ariosto by introducing him here escapes the embarrassment of a lesbian love affair; but he leaves open the question of why Boiardo would have brought us to the brink of such an embarrassment form which the narrative had to escape by a series of such dubious dodges.

What, after all, are the signs that a lesbian relationship bothered Boiardo at al? There are none. Bradamante has a very good idea what's up and comments on it sardonically (stanza 11), but does nothing to open Fiordespina's eyes. In Boiardo's poem, Fiordespina neither whimpers nor frets nor rages, she is queenly throughout. She is not man-crazy, and if she were, she has two immense armies to choose from. Of course it is not within the range of 15th-century possibilities that Fiordespina and Bradamante should form an unchallenged ménage à deux such as might be unremarked common practice in some communities today. But there were, even then, ways of softening the arrangement. Bradamante has recently been badly wounded in battle; Fiordespina might be made to soften somewhat the erotic rage that Ariosto attributes to her, nurse Bradamante back to health, get to know her, and so forth and so on.

(In passing, I must confess that in translating stanza 25, I overstepped the privilege of a translator by having Fiordespina and Bradamante hold hands. I do not know, because Boiardo does not say, if they were afoot or on horseback; if they were on foot, nothing is more likely than that they held hands, though doubtless without the special erotic implications of a song by the Beatles.)

There is special reason to think that Boiardo might have welcomed into his epic a scene of feminine tenderness and compassion. Though he prided himself on having brought Arthurian erotic themes into the military chivalry of the Charlemagne epos, much the greater part of his poem is given over to scenes of savage killing. Women are seen mostly as prizes awarded for successful acts of slaughter; often they fight, not to defend themselves from men, but as warriors in the general cause. An extended scene of female reconcilement might have appeared welcome to the poet's civilized audience — and if it involved a bit of unorthodox sex, which of the ladies in Duke Ercole's court would be likely to object?

Another property of which Boiardo might have anticipated making use to complete Canto Nine was the pair of splendid horses, Andalusian and Irish, of which the ladies disposed. In this enchanted countryside of Boiardo's, with horses of such mettle, they could be within minutes inside some romantic garden or castle which they could explore at will. Bradamante might not be amenable to such an expedition, which in Ariosto's poem has been foreclosed by Merlin's solemn prophecy of her future (Canto Three), but in Boiardo's poem she is still perfectly free to partake of adventures which might be thought unseemly to the foundress of the glorious house of Este.

Two alternatives seem to be precluded: Fiordespina and Bradamante cannot settle down together and live happily ever after. If the king of Spain was ready to burn Riccardietto alive for sleeping with his daughter, how would he have reacted to her settling down with a lesbian partner? Having Fiordespina shift off to a male partner improves matters hardly at all; besides, we have Boiardo's own word that he intended to sing of Fiordespina's love (singular, not plural)"

> *Pèro vi lascio in questo vano amore*
> *Di Fiordespina ardent poco a poco*

He could not have said that if he had already in mind that she would shortly take off with another lover better equipped than Bradamante. Fiordespina's love, though "vano," is said to be "ardente poco a poco" up to the present ending of Canto Nine. It has not yet had time to reach full intensity, so the poet must have intended to it to do so in the future. Yet it dould not be accepted by society or the fascinated listeners of Duke Ercole's court.

What solution then did Boiardo envisage? I think myself that Fiordespina might have seen or might have been made by her creator to see that her passion for Bradamante was destructive of the woman she loved. Recognizing that fact would raise her love to its highest possible point. The couple might and should have had a passionate encounter for a night, a week, a month — a clandestine conjunction — but then, coming back to the "real" world, facing the difficulties of their existence as a couple, Fiordespina might have privately erased herself. I do not know if she would have mentioned the possibility  of this decision to Bradamante. On the whole, I think not. She is a woman of dignity, who would take full responsibility for her own decisions. Perhaps she might have kept about her some keepsake, innocent enough to everyone else, but which would communicate to Bradamante alone the depth of her passion. But this comes close to making a nineteenth-century melodrama out of the story, and on the whole I prefer something more severe. She should make her death appear an accident; only the one person should suspect something otherwise. (I hope she would invent a simple but effective lie which would allow the unhappy campers on the mountainside to pitch their tents and go home before winter sets in.)

Her suicide eliminates her from a plot to which she was never essential; it leaves Bradamante free to pursue her lofty destiny, yet it need not make her appear heartless or cold. It does not allow Fiordespina to look cheap. I flatter myself that Boiardo might have approved.

## FINAL TABLEAU

On a darkened stage, under a dark blue light reminiscent of Fiordespina's gown but not identical with it, a lonely melancholy figure in silver armor and with cropped hair. In the background, very softly, the great theme from *La Forza del Destino*.

◆

# IV *Rue de l'Ancienne Comédie*

### Café Procope,

*blustery November evening of the year 17—*
*Not many customers in the cafe, but promi-*
*nent among them the Abbé Chas Bernard, a*
*plump, spotless ecclesiastic in his middle*
*fifties, sipping every so often at his espresso,*
*but mainly absorbed in his copy of the Mer-*
*cure. Silence: the one elderly waiter seems*
*almost asleep on his feet. Suddenly a clatter*
*from outside and enter, not without a touch*
*of deference, Le Père Adam, shaking a few*
*flakes of snow from his rusty cassock, blowing on his fingers, and bowing to the*
*company, both those present and those imagined. He is slender of person and*
*unassuming, almost humble, of demeanor. Not threadbare, but distinctly*
*travel-worn.*

ABBÉ BERNARD (*looks carefully at the newcomer, seems to recognize him,*
*is briefly in doubt, finally advances to shake him warmly by the hand*): Eh,
Father Adam! How delightful to see you again! I was surprised at first,
thinking you at least a thousand leagues away. But come, warm yourself
at the fire, tell me about yourself. Weren't you in Geneva just recently?

FATHER ADAM (*modestly but not meechingly*): It's a great pleasure for
me to see you again, old friend. As much of a pleasure as it is to be back
in Paris, which we don't really appreciate when we live here all the time.
And how are things with you?

ABBÉ BERNARD: Not well, not badly. Things happen from day to
day, and at the end of the year, what does it amount to? Nothing that
would overflow a teaspoon. Speaking of which, what sort of coffee

would you prefer? Your usual? (*He gestures imperiously to the waiter.*)
How did you leave things at Ferney?

FATHER ADAM:   Well, as you realize, it's not altogether easy to
explain. Ferney can change from day to day or minute to minute; the
household is really like a social whirlwind, within which someone like
myself is no more than a leaf in a storm. Have you heard how I came to
be there in the first place? I thought not; these details don't travel well.
There are a couple of strictly French cafés in Geneva, one of which caters
particularly to players of chess. I went there occasionally, as much to
keep warm of an evening as for love of the game. To tell you the truth,
my friend, I didn't find the competition there very exciting. You know
how it is in a town like that — three or four people know the game, and
if you beat one of them too easily — pfffft! there goes your chance for an
evening's entertainment.

So we played, and I — not to cheat or mislead anyone — let myself
be beaten every so often. Not that I deliberately played badly — mostly
I just kept to myself those gambits which, here at the Procope, once made
a bit of a stir. We played to pass the time, nothing else, and one day M.
de Voltaire wandered by and challenged me. I knew who he was, of
course, and he knew nothing of me but that I was another son of Father
Adam. We played, we divided a few games. It wasn't hard for me to let
him win a couple of times — for a gentleman, he was a pretty fair chess
player. Not good, but clever. Certainly for a casual chess-opponent he
was a very great gentleman. When he invited me to join his household
at Ferney, you would never have guessed that I was a penniless,
unbeneficed priest, and he was a hundred times richer than most of the
crowned heads to whom he loaned money — at an exorbitant interest, so
I'm told. But between us it was very different. I'd be doing him a
particular favor, so he said, by sparing him a journey to town for his
favorite pastime; at Ferney we could play our games *all'improvviso*. And
so forth. You needed only to see the sparkle in his eye to realize that this
was a drollery between us — but so long as it pleased him to keep it up,
it didn't inconvenience me to go along. Quite the contrary. And so I
moved out to Ferney and joined the *ménage* — or better, menagerie —
there.

Don't suppose that life at Ferney didn't have its amenities. It isn't
every period of my life when I could wake up to the gentle rustle of some
little person lighting a fire in my bedroom grate and laying out my
breakfast with the egg properly cooked and a pat of yellow butter for my

roll and the coffee steaming in its pot. And then in the evening, to be sure of one's share of roast beef or baked chicken with currant sauce. That was for us guests — the master lived on the sparest of Carthusian diets: but for us, his guests, it was the land of Cockayne.

ABBÉ BERNARD: You make my mouth water. But, given the pleasures of your situation and the lightness of your duties — why, if I may make so bold, are you suddenly here *chez* Procope, and not, if I may venture a guess from your garb, not in the finest of fettle?

FATHER ADAM: Ever the artful one, aren't you, my friend? No, there's nothing about my stay at Ferney or my departure from that enchanted kingdom that I'm embarrassed to discuss. Though I remained there for only a couple of years, it was the most delightful period of my life, and the most honorable. If only I could give you some idea of what it was like! Ferney, as you know, is in French territory but only a few miles from the city of Geneva, which is of course Swiss. It is a house, rather large for a single gentleman, but not spacious beyond his needs, considering he loves to entertain, and often has fifty or sixty guests of an evening — in addition to which he treats them, every so often, to an evening in the theater, which is a high point of the *soirée*. After the actors have performed, everyone sits down to a modest little opulent supper. And by then it is neither comfortable nor altogether safe to drive back to Geneva in the dark, so the ladies and gentlemen are accommodated in the spare bedrooms, of which there are dozens. Besides these regular theatrical performances, there is an irregular stream of visitors to the house on a semi-regular basis — one or the other of M. de Voltaire's nieces with husband or family, plus a couple of his secretaries, some visiting philosophers, diplomats, historians, poets, biographers, bankers, comedians, buffoons and riffraff like myself, I suppose, whom M. de Voltaire has picked up in his passage through life. Oh, I can't possibly describe to you the flood of people who come pouring through Ferney, sometimes to argue with M. de Voltaire on some point of doctrine or learning, more often just to see him, to be present in the same room with him. During the day he's mostly upstairs, in his bed so I'm told, where he writes, writes, writes; but in the evening he comes down in his big wig and formal suit, and eats a very meager supper, exchanges greetings and jests, consults with the staff, and perhaps plays a game of chess with me. Sometimes he's like the Czar of Russia, icy and distant; sometimes he resembles your dear old uncle Joseph, down from the country for a visit. Oh, if I could only bring before you this parade of the great minds of

Europe, assembled of their own free will to pay homage to a single old man. Plus of course they bring with them an assortment of oddities and entertainers to keep things from getting dull.

*(Father Adam gestures mysteriously, and on the slowly darkening walls of the Procope are projected gradually clarifying images of the élite of Voltaire's "court," on whom Father Adam comments briefly as they pass.)* . . . there is Madame de Fontane, the "quiet" niece (Madame Denis is the plump and most often the noisy one.) Monsieur Bigex is the very small man with glasses; he is M. Voltaire's secretary — the remarkably short, plump man is M. Gibbon, an English historian.

ABBÉ BERNARD *(interrupting):* Isn't that monumental person Marshal Boufflers? I think I saw him once in a parade . . . .

FATHER ADAM *(gaining momentum):* Yes, that's Boufflers. These are just the rich and famous. Mlle Vautiran is just a poor relative, but M. Voltaire always refers to her by a nickname, "Belle et Bonne." and indeed she rules the whole household by those two qualities. M. Covelle, the dry, witty man with a stick, is an oddity within the group. He was accused by the Geneva City Council of committing fornication, admitted the fact, but refused to perform a public act of contrition. M. de Voltaire took him into his household, and had him announced at all dinners and public performances as "M. le Fornicateur." Those are just a few of my friends and associates at Ferney, and for the man who's kicked around the world as I have, they're very congenial. Not too good for comfort, you might say, but not people by whom you need feel yourself degraded. The society grows and shrinks. Some nights we are in the presence of eminence, sometimes of foolishness and games. Outside in the big world things were not always friendly. M. de Voltaire had many enemies at court, who would have liked to get at him, but they were far away, and from Ferney it was only a few miles to Geneva where his French enemies would have no standing.

The Bishop of Annecy was another matter. Ferney lies within his see and over everything that happens at Ferney he exercises — technically, at least — moral jurisdiction. This became important when M. de Voltaire's theatrical performances in Geneva had to be moved, first out of the regular theaters into private homes, and then to Ferney, because the Calvinists objected to them. But them they became so popular at Ferney that long strings of carriages filled the roads every night a performance was announced and the bishop was placed in a humiliating position. Either he forbade his flock to attend the shows, or he advertised to the world that the Catholics at Ferney were more lax, morally, than the Protestants in Geneva.

ABBÉ BERNARD: And were they? Pardon me for asking, but I suppose we ought to be quite clear . . . .

FATHER ADAM: My dear fellow, of course they were not. Plays by Corneille and Racine, shown many years ago before the royal court, and now revived before an audience of Geneva bankers and gentry — as stiff and proper as you could want! No, my friend, you'd find more immorality on one little back alley of Paris than in all the theatrical performances mounted in Ferney for years on end. Still, one doesn't need much of an occasion to start a quarrel between irritable people. M. de Voltaire was determined to provoke the bishop, as the bishop was out to humble M. de Voltaire; as for morality, there was as little care for it on the one side as on the other. But see now how things worked out.

The bishop from his palace at Annecy denounced the theatrical performances being staged at Ferney. M. de Voltaire, as anyone could have anticipated, continued to stage and advertise them. And the more the clergy of both parties denounced them, the more the populace continued to think the stage performances must be wicked and intriguing spectacles indeed. They flocked to attend. The bishop ordered the parish priest, M. Boildeau, who is the meekest and mildest of men, to punish M. Voltaire for his contumacy. Only one punishment lay within the priest's power, which was to cut off the disobedient parishioner from communion. That was what was expected of M. Boildeau, and that, with much trepidation, he actually did or vowed to do.

Only think, if you will, if this didn't stir up a hornet's nest in our little village. The church stands on land donated by M. de Voltaire; it was built with his money. On its pediment it carries in splendid letters the inscription DEO EREXIT VOLTAIRE.

ABBÉ BERNARD (drily): Yes, I've heard of that inscription, with God getting a good deal less prominence than the donor. Tell me, my friend, is there anywhere in the Christian world such a reversal of things, where the creator of the entire universe is more openly humbled beneath the conceit of one of his creations?

FATHER ADAM (visibly taken aback by this outburst, but not silenced): I'm delighted, my dear fellow, that we've reached the crux of the matter so quickly. We should be over it in just a few more moments more. For let me assure you that what began as a rural comedy, has ended by disturbing me greatly, and I hope you will be able to help me to settle my mind on a host of matters.

We had an impasse then — the bishop determined to rebuke M. de Voltaire, M. de Voltaire resisting rebuke. Both men as proud as Lucifer; and between them, poor M. Boildeau, the parish priest, trembling, placatory, helpless. Voltaire moved first. One morning he did not come down to breakfast; there were anxious queries. M. de Voltaire is so thin as a rule that when he sets aside even a bit of toast, there is cause for concern. The next word was that he had a cough. Nobody heard it, but his valet spread the word. Ferney has a northern, a distinctly northern pattern of weather. He spent the day in his bedroom, and in the evening let it be known that he was feeling better — better than what, he did not say. But he did not come down for dinner, as had been his wont, and word was that his cough was no better.

The health of a man like M. de Voltaire is fragile at best. He is so painfully thin that when he eats a fillet of lake trout or a wing of chicken, it is cause for rejoicing. When the doctor is summoned, the whole household goes into mourning. It was with mounting trepidation that we followed the bulletins from the bedroom. But the real shock came on the fifth day, with word that the parish priest had been summoned. We did not know if he would respond — did not know if the bishop's ban would be upheld in the hour of supreme crisis. Poor M. Boildeau was beside himself. Nobody doubted that he wanted to administer the sacraments; he was in his meek and dutiful way utterly devoted to M. de Voltaire. He did not think, any more than any other civilized person would think, that the church should lay a blight on one of its children for providing a harmless entertainment for some of his friends. On the other hand, directly defying the orders of one's bishop — what sort of church discipline could there be if that sort of thing was condoned?

ABBÉ BERNARD: Shocking, shocking. The quarrel itself was bad enough; but to have it spread through society, and be argued on the public streets! For I don't suppose either side made any effort to keep it quiet.

FATHER ADAM: No effort at all. The peasants on M. de Voltaire's estates, the workers in his watch factories, the salesmen of his silk stockings took up the cause of the *patron* and argued his rights, whether or not they knew what the inside of a theater looked like. If the bishop had tried to visit Ferney, he'd have been lucky to escape with his life. Then one day the fateful call arrived from the committee of doctors assembled by M. de Voltaire's bedside. The patient was worse, much worse, his condition was despaired of. The priest was summoned, and the priest arrived, white and shaking, looking himself like an invalid on his deathbed. You can imagine the turmoil in the household — not just in the crowd clustered around the bedroom door, but up and down the hallways, in the kitchens, and outside in the stables and barns. M. de Voltaire had been a generous patron. If I tell you he was much loved, that sounds cynical, for of course servants love a generous master, but they also love a humane and a kindly employer. A lot of the Ferney people had been on the estate for years, and remembered unexpected gratuities, holidays, donatives. Some of them loved M. de Voltaire as a man, and would have been sorry to see him die. Others just knew he was an important person, but still he was their support, their living. And there were still others — I am sorry to say this — who knew he was the enemy of the church, and held the church responsible for his death. Foolish and uninformed men, of course. But men of simple, uninformed prejudices and loyalties. I have seen them grind their teeth as a priest passed; I have felt the glare of their eyes turned on me. Even those who did not love M. de Voltaire, or had no reason to do so, hated the church which denied him salvation for no better reason than the upholding of its own pride and dignity. Their authority for these views was not a book, not a preacher, but that terrible shapeless figure called "everybody." Not everybody hated the church, but everybody of a certain class and social position did, and I don't have to tell you how demoralizing that is.

Well, so matters stood on the morning of Friday, September 27, when suddenly from upstairs around the door of the sickroom there was an explosion of violent and completely incoherent noise. There were cries of joy — apparently the patient had recovered. There were loud guffaws and belly-laughs. There were cries of surprise, shouts of what could have been anger. Everything except the reserved melancholy that should have accompanied the last rites of the church. The anger could have been taken to mean that the patient had died without the last rites. Some people were openly weeping. And suddenly here he is, not only alive but apparently well, resting one hand on the shoulder of his old friend the parish priest, and speaking as from a rostrum to the crowd of servants and guests on the floor below, I can't pretend to give you his exact words, but the substance of them was this:

"I'm much touched, my dear friends, to see your anxiety and concern over my condition. It's true that I've not felt well for the last few days, and yesterday I even called for my old friend Father Boildeau, to check over the state of my soul and see if it was prepared for the long voyage it might be called on to undertake. Father Boildeau not only gave me a clean bill of spiritual health, he so encouraged my soul that I've decided to postpone my long voyage for a while. So if you'll make way a bit on the stairs here, I shall come down and breakfast on the hot cup of coffee and elegant brioches that they prepare so well at Ferney."

And so he carried it off. The household applauded as he ate his breakfast. The parson looked like an alley cat that had just been drenched in a bucket of fish-oil. (I think he already heard, ringing through his ears, the bitter scoldings he would soon endure from the bishop.) But the deed was done; M. de Voltaire had received the absolution to which he was not entitled; punishment for staging theatrical productions was forgotten, the whole notion of ecclesiastical authority over M. de Voltaire was reduced to a joke.

ABBÉ BERNARD: And so you left his employ — if that's the word for it. And quite rightly, my dear Father Adam. When the power figures start fighting with one another, so that the only result is scandal, there's nothing for us little people to do but to get out of the way.

FATHER ADAM: I'm afraid your reaction means mostly that I haven't presented my story very well. Between you and me, I felt less than no sympathy for the Bishop of Annecy. This wasn't a personal matter, though in fact I could not abide the man. He was never kind to me, though he knew I came to see him dirt-poor and in search of any honorable position. I say I didn't like him, and in fact I never did; but I didn't say I couldn't like him because I probably could. Just as with the servants of M. de Voltaire, if he had done something for me, I might have felt more warmly toward him. But tell me, my dear fellow, isn't that horrible footing on which to put human relations?

There is a notion that's been creeping up on me very gradually, but it deepens as it persists, and I put it before you as an old friend because its presence worries me. I don't see where it may lead; I don't know how to get rid of it. Very simply, it is that rules, laws, and general prescriptions encourage people to behave worse than otherwise they would do. In this recent squabble, you couldn't find if you looked for them two men more different by temperament and training than M. de Voltaire and the Bishop of Annecy. Yet they jog along comfortably enough till one tries to lay down laws for the other. Probably they are good laws in their import and intent — good too, or at least harmless, in their general application.

Not everybody has enough money to build a theater in his private house — or enough interest in the theater. So regulation of the theaters applies only to a few rich amateurs — as a matter of fact, only to one. Besides, regulation and censorship are only one path to control of theaters. There is the power of taxation, which can be brought to bear, in ways I need not detail. There is public opinion to be mobilized — what else does the power of the pulpit amount to?

All sorts of ways for the Bishop to protect his congregation from the corrupting influence of a theater which they need not even enter if they don't want to. But is that the only function of a Bishop, or for that matter of a clergy? One of my wandering thoughts is that a morality which is quite appropriate for the Haute Savoie may be too restrictive by half for the residents of a city like Geneva. Or restrictive in the wrong way. A farmer on the upland meadows can't be treated as if he were a cosmo-politan capitalist like M. de Voltaire — and vice-versa.

ABBÉ BERNARD: *Especially* vice-versa. A bishop of the church can't be treated as if he were an itinerant mendicant moralist intruding like an unwanted foreigner in his own see. We understand these matters well enough, most of us, in most circumstances. Our rules and regulations are formulated strictly, categorically. Your M. de Voltaire, who is just little Arouet, transformed by an anagram and an immense pile of money into a *bourgeois gentilhomme*, could be exempt from the rules and observe the forms — that is, talk privately with one of the bishop's chaplains and let it be known what he wants and how much he is willing to contribute to the bishop's favorite charity. They talk, they chuckle; they exchange confidences. Nothing is transacted in the way of business, but agree-ments are reached with or without the use of words. In a little while differences that would require a volume of legal terminology are smoothed over. M. de Voltaire is allowed to do most of what he wants, the bishop's dignity is preserved. The law — if there is one — does not say, "No theaters under penalty of so and so," but rather, "No exhibitions in very bad taste," or "No exhibitions which might offend public morality." And each of these phrases is subject to interpretation by lawyers whose interpretations of each others' interpretations can be prolonged till the Greek kalends. Don't look so disturbed, old friend — that's how the world mostly goes. People of principle get into flashy flights, but in the end most of them wind up in tangled compromises.

FATHER ADAM (*with a sigh*): I dare say. You're a man of more experiences in the world than I, and no doubt you're right. But why then do we have all these wretched rules and misleading regulations, which don't mean what they say or what they mean, in the first place.

ABBÉ BERNARD: As reminders, mostly. There are so many directives and forbiddings and particular exceptions that we have to have some broad, simple laws and sweeping principles that people can remember and anticipate. Don't steal the apple off the pushcart or you'll get whacked. You don't have to steal twenty apples and get whacked twenty times before the idea starts to sink in. Rules are made, in a word, not to be obeyed, but to be remembered. Plain, direct rules repeated over and over again, with a whack every so often to remind one that there's a penalty attached to disobedience. It's all part of the process of training people into thinking they want what in fact they don't want at all. You are horrified at the cruelty of the process. Dear Father Adam, your feelings do the very greatest credit to your good heart. But with all our efforts — by "our" I mean not just churchmen but magistrates and gendarmes and jailers and hangmen and headsmen — with all these combined efforts to make men behave — look at the world as it is!

So we have to pretend to frighten M. de Voltaire — not that I suppose for an instant that he lost a minute's sleep over the whole matter — and not that he and his pretty little theater and his glittering clientele matter a rap — but because of the canaille that lurk behind him. Who are they? Step with me just a few blocks away to the Place Pigalle, and you can inspect a fine collection of them. Pimps and pornographers and peep-show artists, Every sort of filth and indecency for anybody who has two sous and an idle minute. Try as they may, the church and the society can do nothing to dry up this swamp of corrupt squalor because it springs from the corrupt heart of man.

FATHER ADAM: We're back to basics, aren't we? I'm sorry that our conversation has taken on such a symbolic and almost cosmic dimension. We started by talking of two men who have quarrelled and in their quarrel have tried to hurt and humiliate one another. We wind up discussing the origins of evil and the natural goodness or badness of man. But apparently it's inevitable. Everyone reaches after a principle or source of authority, and the impression that he possesses such authority makes the original partisan ever more dogmatic. With words, with swords, with guns, and with fire men try to impose on their fellow men behavior patterns that the stronger group prefers. And thus most of the words used under these circumstances, words like justice and morality — all the good-bad words — are nothing but shallow deceptions, used to cover up the force we ultimately rely on.

You imply that I left the house of M. de Voltaire at Ferney in holy horror at the evil views being promulgated there. I don't think that's the way it was. My fellow-clergyman, M. Boildeau, had been publicly humiliated, to the point where I could barely look into his miserable shame ridden face. The Bishop of Annecy, who had never liked or trusted me, was by now my bitter enemy. And the jocose jesters who congratulated me on M. de Voltaire's "victory," (as if I had somehow had a hand in it) — these loud libertines actually turned my stomach. It had been like a war, and it left everyone savage and sore.

For M. de Voltaire, in whose nature I think I could recognize the marks of an original disposition, there are perhaps excuses to be made. His weapons, like those of a weasel, are teeth and claws, faster, sharper, and more vicious than those of any other animal. He has lived by them all his life. If he ever had a compelling example of charity, I never heard of it. But I think the Bishop of Annecy should have set a better example for one whose sharp tongue and sarcastic temper he knew of old. He was provoked, sure enough, but isn't there something in the good book about turning the other cheek? Still, I pass no judgement on the parties; between them, my life at Ferney was impossible. I made my farewells to the household and the master of it; he was generous at our last meeting beyond all my expectations. I am glad to have had the experience, and glad to be out of it all.

ABBÉ BERNARD: And where do you turn now, my friend? For I don't think your present views are likely to be well received in the church. I wish I could offer you, for a time, a room in my modest abode, but. . . .

FATHER ADAM: Don't even think of it, old friend. I couldn't consider it. Besides, there's no need. I took care of myself very well before I crossed the border into Switzerland, and I can do so again.

ABBÉ BERNARD: But where? How?

FATHER ADAM: You forget, old friend, that there's one art in which I am practiced beyond any other mortal man.

ABBÉ BERNARD (who can do nothing but sputter):  ???? but!!!!

FATHER ADAM:  Nobody in Paris has had half the practice I've received in the art of losing chess games gracefully. Don't imagine that there's anything simple in my art. The first undercoat of my picture is laid down in the course of the game itself — it's a mixture of admiration for the opponent which can't be a shade too obvious, with chagrin over one's own mistakes which also can't be in the least forced. Oh, it's a performance that I've practiced many times over the years, have re-hearsed before the mirror late into the night. I couldn't do it here in the Procope, of course — too many people know me. But there are enough cafés in the city and enough cities in the country to provide game for my modest chase over the next few years. Which are all either of us need to worry about, right? So let me thank you for the cup of coffee, and ask of you one favor: if you see me playing chess around town here, there, or anywhere, please don't recognize me. It would be a supreme kindness.

*He rises, redeems his tattered soutane, and exits into the snow.*

◆

# V CAGOTS

he district of Baigorry, though its name gives the fleeting impression of an Irish expletive, is geographically located in the French *département* of the Basses-Pyrénées, with the Spanish border just to the south and the Bay of Biscay some miles off to the west. Baigorry (which is actually the name of a prehistoric Basque divinity) lies in the first foothills of the Pyrenees themselves. It is a countryside of rolling hills and easy hollows; the mountains proper begin just to the south. Though by no means awe-inspiring peaks at this end of the range, they offer plenty of narrow defiles, steep cliffs, and precarious roadways which define a difficult boundary. Just a few miles over the border in Spain is the ancient abbey of Roncevaux, which preserves in its name, if nowhere else, the memory of Roland, Oliver, and their heroic rear-guard stand against overwhelming hordes of savage Saracens. (That's all in the poem, of course; modern historians seem to have decided that the "Saracen hordes" were in fact a scattering of Basque tribesmen interested mainly in loot.) However that may be, Roncevaux the Abbey survives with its memories, though they are mostly of a later, unsung hero, Pedro II the Strong (1174-1213), whose tomb and trophies occupy positions of prominence in the *sala capitular*. Baigorry itself has had little to worry about for the last millennium or so, whether from incursions by Saracens, Spaniards, tourists, or anybody else. A sizeable element of Basques remains on the land, where they have been from time immemorial; they preserve their language, their national game of fronton, their dreams of an ultimate unified Basque population (Euzkadi). But separatism does not seem a pressing problem any more than invasion. Lying directly on a useful but minor pilgrimage route to Compostela, the inhabitants of Baigorry have always profited more from peace than war, and never seem to have thought of laying out their major town for defense. The community is strung out along a couple of intersecting roads quite open to the surrounding countryside. There is a church at the crossroads which has been standing there so long, it has given its name to the community as a whole: Saint Etienne de Baigorry. Laid back and tolerant like the rest of this agricultural community, it has resolved its linguistic dilemmas by offering services and hymnals in both languages, French and Basque; pick your spot on the schedule, and you can attend the service in the language of your choice. The problem has not been solved, not by a long shot, but the rough edges have been worn off it.

The fabric of the church is quite old, dating, as local annals tell us, from the thirteenth century; but there are surprises inside. Some time in the eighteenth century a builder who had clearly been impressed by a metropolitan stage-theater fitted out Saint Etienne with three sets of wooden galleries, almost like banks of loges, which run down the sides of the nave. They increase the seating capacity of the church; they may have divided the congregation into classes; they certainly placed most of the auditors on a higher plane, physically, than the celebrant. In most churches the hearers sit at ground level while the preacher speaks to them from above — his pulpit is a sort of eminence. Not so in Saint Etienne's. The impression is not displeasing, but it can be surprising.

A second feature of the church — even more curious if less obtrusive — is a small sealed entry set in the right-hand wall of the nave only a little forward of the main porch and door. It is quite a small entry; only one individual could get in at a time, and he would have to crouch. Three very well-worn stone steps lead from it down to the floor of the church. It is explained as the door of the cagots (with a soft *g* as in *rouge*); and the printed sheet describing the church invites one to note also, beside the door, the special font or stoup for holding the holy water distributed to cagots, and to cagots only. The "regular" congregation had a font of their own, larger and more handsome, near the front of the church.

Who, then, were these cagots, these second-class Christians in the land of the Most Christian King? It is a relatively late name for a special small parish group, found most commonly (though not exclusively) in southwestern France, and defined most strikingly by its rigid exclusion from the life of the general community. As a separate group, cagots no longer exist, having died out or merged into the society of their neighbors during the nineteenth century. There remain a few descendants of cagots, some records and remnants of cagots (as in the church of Saint Etienne), as well as a few villages that used to be inhabited predominantly by cagots. But of cagots themselves there are none.

The old question used to be, Where did they come from? and the best modern answer is undoubtedly that nobody knows. "Cagot" is a sixteenth-century name for people who were marked out as distinctive at least several centuries before that. One of the very early names carries on its face a big question mark: they were called *crestiaas* or in the Latin *christiani*. Why specify as "christians" people apparently admitted to the church only under special and somewhat humiliating conditions? Evidently, like other outcasts and people afflicted with incurable diseases, they fell under the special, if ambiguous, protection of the church. Being forbidden to own property, they could not be sued at civil law; being very often mendicants, they had a special claim on the charity of the church; and being menaces (real or imagined) to the public health, they might be confined with all the other incurables — the insane, the leprous, the sufferers from erysipelas and from Saint Vitus's dance — in the catchall jails/hospitals/lazar-houses/hospices of the monasteries. But on the other hand, when they were without visible symptoms of any disease, they were often urged to move out to save space for other patients by begging their bread or doing specially assigned menial work on the outside. Thus to the common mind they could be *crestiaas* (with a tacit implication of being lepers or as good as ) while enjoying the privileges of neglect, penury, and social ostracism in the world at large.

Identification of cagots with lepers was further fostered by an unhappily applied Biblical story which crystallized into yet another name for the wretched outcasts; they were called Giezetains after Gehazi, the servant of Elisha the Prophet (II Kings, 5). The story was brief, its application deadly. Naaman, a captain of the Syrian army, came to Elisha to be healed of leprosy. After the miracle the prophet would accept no reward, but his servant Gehazi went after the cured Naaman and, on his own, collected money. Elisha naturally knew about it at once (no use trying to keep secrets from a prophet), and transferred Naaman's leprosy to Gehazi. Elisha was not, in fact, the sort of prophet who did things by halves; some boys who twitted him on his baldness found that out when the prophet called out of the forest a couple of bears who killed and ate forty-two boys (II Kings 2, 23-24). And so the curse on Gehazi applied not only to him but "to his seed forever." That meant, for the clergy of the eleventh and twelfth centuries, the cagots. Their connection with Gehazi, who lived three thousand years before and two thousand miles away, could be taken for granted.

One difficulty presented itself, to be sure, in that the cagots showed no symptoms of leprosy; but the theological conclusion to be drawn was that they showed no outer signs of the disease because, like Gehazi, they were incurably corrupt within. Had they been honest lepers, they would have exhibited all the loathsome signs of their disease, but they were such consummate hypocrites that they let nothing appear. Their seeming innocence masked the deepest and darkest corruption of all. When this story began to wear thin, a phantom disease called "white leprosy" was invented, with a great variety of different and difficult symptoms. But all these medical fantasies (some of which appeared in medical textbooks until just a few years ago) were founded on the radical and utterly erroneous assumption that leprosy is an inherited disease. It is not. It is the product of a specific organism, *Bacillus leprae*. it is transmitted by prolonged contact, and develops into a pathological condition only after an extended period of incubation; it cannot descend genetically from Gehazi or anybody else. Children of real lepers may pick up the disease, but it is by contact, generally under insanitary conditions, not by inheritance. Thus all the notions (too many even to enumerate) that the cagots were a separate tribe or even a peculiar "race" fall under the head of popular delusions.

Folk-etymologies frequently lent a helping hand to these delusions; for example, the word "cagot" was solemnly analyzed as a modified form of "chasse-Goths," or "Goth-chasers." Isolated groups of Saracens were supposed to have got lost in the mountains while chasing the Goths out of Spain, and to have developed weird physical symptoms while hiding out over the centuries. Just as popular was the belief that the cagots were themselves vestigial Visigoths. But the word "cagot" itself makes no appearance till the sixteenth century, and as the last Goths left Spain some eight hundred years before, the supposed etymologies, apart form being ridiculous, are irrelevant.

Even the notion that they were a separate, exotic race did not help the cagots, for they were thought to be a nation under a special divine curse, so whatever merit was implicit in the name of "crestiaas" or "Christians" was abrogated for them. In the high Alps hundreds of miles to the east, goitrous individuals were known for a time, not unkindly, as "chretiens," from which we inherit the word "cretin." The implication was that despite their horrible disabilities (which we know nowadays are prevented by a touch of iodine in the diet), they too had Christian souls. But the crestiaas-cagots of southwest France were never seen in this kindly light; spawn of an evil principle, they were evil themselves, therefore to be hated and rejected.

Supervised quarantine of those suffering from real leprosy is not always an inhumane practice; but for the cagots, who were not lepers at all, their treatment amounted to a cruel and superstitious shunning. Fearful stories about them proliferated. They were said to have had little tails on their backsides and blotches (of presumably diabolic origin) under their armpits, they had no ear-lobes, they stank abominably, they were unnaturally (and of course deliciously) lustful, their hands were misshapen in the likeness of claws, their mere touch withered and blighted living things. All these alleged deformities and malign influences could easily have been investigated and proved false; but the stories generated other stories, not so easy to wash away. The provincial countryside possessed its normal quota of physical and mental defectives — half-wits, cripples, epileptics, sufferers from birth defects — many of whom might be cured nowadays and admitted to a "normal" existence. But the easiest and cheapest way to dispose of them four or five hundred years ago was to label them "cagots," force them to wear an ugly red badge in the likeness of a goose-foot, and dump them in a rural slum, where the afflictions of some could be attributed to all.

Thus many of them disappeared into the maquis, building themselves little hut villages, usually beyond a stream of purifying water or in the depths of a forest. Their isolation contributed to the variety of names by which they went. Some regions knew them as cagots, others called them capots, cahets, gahots, agotes, caquets, cacous, caquins, gafets, and gafas. Some of these names were contemptuous and offensive, others merely colloquial. But because the cagots did not move around very much, the names tended to stick where they were given. By necessity or choice or a mixture of both, cagots tended to live outside towns, in the neighborhood of a church, a monastery, or a nobleman's castle, but in a any case mostly by themselves. They settled predominantly in the plains or piedmonts, much less often in the mountain valleys. (That might have disposed of the story that they were residual Saracens who had got stuck in the mountain fastnesses — that and the fact that in spite of the many discouragements they remained assiduous church-goers.) A few managed to settle in cities as big as Bordeaux, where they were confined to ghettos know as "cagotteries." The one trait which distinguished them everywhere — though everywhere it took slightly different forms — was their segregation.

They could not own land, practice any of the trades or professions, handle food at the markets (even what they had grown or gathered themselves), could not carry weapons, enter the church by the regular door, stand in any but the assigned place, or receive communion before any "clean" person. Often the wafer was handed to them at the end of a cleft stick; sometimes it was merely tossed to them through the air. Their holy water was kept in a separate font. Never were they allowed to kiss the *porte-paix* or *pax* until all the "clean" members of the congregation had done so, lest in the affirmation itself of brotherhood they spread contamination. They could not practice any craft other than the one specifically prescribed for them: in the south it was woodcutting or carpentry, further north in Britanny it was rope-making. To keep them from befouling the public earth, they were obliged to wear shoes when out walking, and on their outer garment they were required to display the red badge of a goose's foot. In some districts, where superstition was extreme, they were supposed to carry the warning rattle or *cliquetis*, with which lepers alerted passers-by to their approach. Very widespread and deeply felt, though purely superstitious, was the taboo on burying a dead cagot in the common graveyard. The body had to be taken to a segregated cemetery, and violations, or attempted violations, of this posthumous discrimination led to many communal riots, some as late as the closing years of the seventeenth century.

Though they were poor, few uneducated, isolated, and confronted by a wall of united secular and religious authority backed by widespread public animosity against them, the cagots mounted some sporadic protests against their conditions. Fist fights took place in the church when cagots were pushed back into their traditional positions of inferiority. The authorities passed and repassed regulations limiting the cagots' economic activity — a clear sign that the established rules were being ignored or transgressed. Since the professions were too "clean" to touch them, it was inevitable that some cagots picked up the rudiments of law and even of medicine on order to practice within their own community. In an intimate family situation involving the most fearsome taboo of all, that against intermarriage, there was not much to be done. As late as the latter eighteenth century, a bold cagot took the bull by the horns and asked his girl's father if he could marry her, "clean" though she was.

Predictably the old man said No. "Well," said the suitor, "you'd better give us your blessing anyhow because she's already pregnant, and by me." But the father said he'd rather have a bastard in the family than a cagot for a son-in-law; and that was that. Prejudice among the peasantry could be rock-hard.

On the other hand, the higher the authority to which they appealed, the better the cagots appeared to fare. As early as 1514 the agotes of northern Spain petitioned Pope Leo X that they were being denied their proper place in the church, and got a promise of redress. But something not very mysterious happened to the official documents on their way through the episcopal machinery in Pamplona, so nothing resulted. In 1520 the agotes tried again, this time with the Emperor Charles V, to the same benevolent and empty effect. In 1684, following up on ineffectual petitions of 1562 and 1611, the cagots in France were finally able to extract from Louis XIV letters patent which not only achieved registration by the appropriate parlements but actually provided a perceptible fine for anyone who should insult or humiliate the cagots by applying derogatory names to them. Thus after more than a century of agitation, complaint, and silent suffering, something was achieved. In parish documents and municipal records the offensive code-word giezetain, meaning "leper," was replaced by the less obvious code-word *charpentier*, meaning woodworker, meaning "leper."

Slow and small as it was, the movement of officialdom reflected important changes earlier in the century. For the first time in 1600, under orders from the parlement of Toulouse, a team of medical men (two professors of medicine and two practicing physicians) directly examined a couple of dozen randomly chosen cagots. Inspired by this bold example, the parlement of Bordeaux ordered a similar inquiry, and in 1611 two physicians of Béarn examined the cagots of that district as well. In every instance the examining physicians reported unanimously that the cagots they inspected were in a perfect state of health. No trace of leprosy was found, whether white, spotted, or any other variety. The cagots had no infectious diseases at all. That might have been thought to settle the matter, and in the edict of 1684 the judgement of the doctors did no doubt exercise some influence. But ancient traditions died hard, and there were some impressive authorities on the other side. What to do when one read in the authoritative medical treatises of Ambroise Paré (collected, 1575) about cagots so profoundly poisonous that one of them, simply by holding a ripe apple in his hand for an hour, could shrivel it to a dry husk? If one believed the much less distinguished doctors of 1600 and 1611, Paré, the pride of French medical practice, the most distinguished surgeon of his day, had lent his name to a farrago of ignorant claptrap. In fact, he had; but to say so straight out was not easy. And in any case, the problem lay not in the learned classes or with the readers of learned treatises, it was rooted in the popular mind.

Southern France, in that corner between the Pyrenees and the sea, was an isolated community, backward socially, economically, and intellectually. Mountains and marshes kept the people isolated; the main commercial route to Spain ran to the east through the province of the commercially-minded Catalonians. For centuries the teaching of the church, dominated by the vindictive words of Elisha, had belabored the insidious wickedness of the cagots. From these teachings, as from equivalent prejudices about witches, Gypsies, Jews, and other pariahs, some at least of the gentry considered themselves more or less emancipated. They were too far above the cagots to bother hating them; and besides, to big landowners, who were commonly military leaders as well, the cagots could be useful. At harvest time, or in the middle of a big building project, cagots provided a ready reservoir of cheap and frequently of skilled workers. Where, as in many districts of Béarn and Gascony, they practically monopolized the carpenter's trade, the substantial amount of woodwork involved in making, for example, a bridge or a castle had to be assigned to these outcasts. When he raised the fortress of Montanar in 1379, the famous Gaston Phebus Comte de Foix signed (through his agents) a contract with ninety-eight *crestiaas*, representing the entire cagot population of Béarn, to do all the wood- and ironwork on the structure.

(The unique document for the construction of Montanar is of more than passing interest; it shows that the cagots of Béarn had a corporate identity and some sort of communal authority which could allot portions of the global payment to individuals according to the value of the work they performed. The ninety-eight signatories were not the entire *crestiaa* population of Béarn, but signed in the name of all, as representatives. That they had to be contracted for shows further that they could not be drafted or otherwise coopted involuntarily.)

What the Comte de Foix did on a grand scale, lesser gentry found proportionately convenient. In military operations, where wagons, weapons, and siege machines had to be built and repaired, separate companies of cagots might be recruited. They objected as religious paupers to serving in the regular armies; an exemption was granted as an extension of their privilege from paying taxes, i.e., *taille*. But they got paid for their work, and after the campaign was over, some of them might well accompany the commander back to his chateau to refurbish his salon, pavilion, or whatever. For such and similar reasons, cagots might sometimes count on more sympathy from the upper classes than from the "clean" of their humble neighbors.

Hostility from the peasantry should not have been a matter of direct competition for the land, which cagots could not legally own; it could not have stemmed from jealously of privileges, of which both groups had precious few. When shoving-matches between cagots and their enemies broke out, it was frequently over precedence at church services — that is, from fear of infection by contact — or over the purely symbolic issue of burial rights. The compromise which grudgingly admitted cagots by a side entrance to the back of the church — wretched as it was — could not be applied to the cemetery. In 1687 a deceased cord-maker of Pluvigny in Brittany was to be buried, at the request of her family, in the parish church. She was one of the cageaux, or Breton cagots, who had attended the church all her life long without causing controversy. But in death the church could not protect her. The parish priest was not only enlightened but perfectly brave, for he went boldly ahead with the ceremony. (Perhaps he was a little ignorant as well; the peasantry made a point of the fact that he was "not of the country.") But the congregation formed a solid bloc to turn back the cortège, drove off the mourners, upset the coffin, and flung the corpse into a ditch.

Nor was that the end of the matter. Next time one of the pariah group died, and the same headstrong minister wanted to inter the body in the regular cemetery, secular authorities (i.e., armed soldiers) accompanied the corpse. But once again, they were stoned, menaced, vilified, and lucky to escape with their lives. This was mob violence that the law could not condone; in due course, two of the ringleaders were tried, condemned, and ceremoniously hanged in the public square. At different times and in different districts of France, similar and even worse scenes were repeated. Dead bodies were secretly exhumed, graves desecrated, screaming women turned religious services into a banshee's hullaballoo.

Hatred of such dimensions — deep, incoherent, murderous — takes most of the juice out of that primeval question of where the cagots came from. Country people sometimes used to say, with bleary satisfac-

tion, "there was a big battle long ago, and all the losers became cagots."
Dumb it might be, but that was a more satisfactory answer than you
could get by asking if they were Goths or Goth-chasers, descendants of
Gehazi, or sufferers from the purely imaginary ailment of "white leprosy." Some people thought they might be refugee Albigensians, lost or
abandoned members of pilgrimage trains, leftover reformers or crusad-
ers, or simple outlaw bands. The latest suggestion, though ingenious, is
surely one of the weakest. M. Alain Guerreau and Yves Guys (*Les Cagots
du Béarn*, Minerve, 1988) propose that because primogeniture was unusually strict in the Pyrenees piedmont, dispossessed younger sons
struck off on their own and became cagots. But at a time when cagots
were presumed to be lepers, the whole family must have known that the
new cagots were not lepers at all, just younger sons. Why would they
have wanted to blacken the family name with this malignant and improbable story? M. Guerreau modifies his thesis on p. 205 to make the
cagots, rather doubtfully, "cadets? valets? artisans" — in other words, a
miscellaneous band of outcasts. Which leaves us about where we were.

But in fact none of the origin-speculation matters at all. The fact
that they were pariahs and outcasts preceded all explanations of why
they were pariahs and outcasts. Very often the hatred was its own cause,
often it preceded and sometimes it created its own evidence. It was not
rational, did not depend on proofs, could not be overcome by arguments, documents, or tangible evidence. Public prejudice drew a veil of
fantasy before the learned eye of Ambroise Paré; and one Florimond de
Roemond, writing in 1599, hung his own argument out to dry by
observing that cagots were separated in church, *therefore* they must smell
bad, *doubtless* due to some form of infection, *most probably* a variety of
leprosy. With such a string of connectives, one could prove that any
group of outcasts was afflicted with any conceivable disease. Hatred
blurred the vision of eye-witnesses like the observer writing in the
middle of the enlightened nineteenth century, who asserted that in the
Pyrenees "one notes in the most miserable quarters of the town shapeless creatures with swollen and wobbly heads, twisted legs, feeble
bodies, goitrous necks, dull vague eyes, and incoherent speech. Such are
the cagots! Everything points to their Visigothic origin, their name itself
is evidence. . . ." (Cenac Moncaut, *Histoire des Pyrénées* (Paris, Amyot,
1853) V, 262 ff.) Less prejudiced witnesses tell a very different story. Not
all cagots looked alike. Those living near Saint Etienne were dark, dour,
and sickly (their huts had been built in a swamp); but those living near

Saint Jean Pied-de-Port just a few miles away were blonde, active, and musically inclined. For sure, Gaston de Foix did not hire to build his castle specimens like those palsied phantoms who haunted the vision of Monsieur Moncaut. Fewer than twenty-five years after publication of this fearsome portrait, the cagots had melted so thoroughly into the general population that they could no longer be seen anywhere, or, if seen, recognized. (And, in passing, a word has to be said in behalf of the Visigoths, who were by no means cretinous degenerates. Ammianus Marcellinus speaks of them with terror as brutal and heartless beasts, Bishop Orosius praises them as humane and generous conquerors, but nobody ever scorned them as weaklings. They were Arians, to be sure, but not zanys.)

As with so many other institutions, the French Revolution truncated the cagot system (so to speak) with an abruptness which after a millennium of silent disregard and disintegration was more apparent than real. The cagots vanished because they were eager to do so, and because they were different from the regular population only in being segregated. When they were no longer segregated, they no longer existed as a group because they spoke the same dialects as their neighbors, worshipped at the same church, observed most of the same customs, and had suffered the same tribulations as Frenchmen at large, along with a few extras. Social disorder had for hundreds of years been mixing social groups together, not indiscriminately but profusely. During the sixteenth-century religious wars, of which Montaigne has left such a vivid account, gangs of blood-thirsty, booty-crazed ruffians roamed the countryside; which of them had the imagination to wonder whether he was stealing chickens or abducting sheep from cagots or somebody else? if anything, being a pariah was a real advantage for anyone trying to survive the civil wars. At that time, many cagots, ex-cagots, and even the "clean" deliberately picked up the badges of a leper's shame, and flaunted them in public view. With looters and plunderers running wild in the land, to be considered a deadly health risk was as good as an insurance policy — especially since one didn't have to be an actual leper.

Thus social disorder and legal anomalies had for years been facilitating the escape of cagots from their state of humiliating inferiority. Some quietly migrated to districts where their previous status was unknown, others left the country entirely. The solitary life of a sheep herder brought some to the mountains of northwest Spain, and from there, further, to the deserts of western America. Very rarely, and only late in the history of the group, did a cagots rise to such eminence that his disgraceful origins could be safely advertised. The most notable instance was Betrand DuFresne (1736-1801), a cagot by birth, who rose high in the civil service and achieved under Napoleon an honorable position in the national administration. The policy of a *carrière ouverte aux talents* was just what the cagot needed, exactly what they had been pleading for, century after weary century. Some of them undoubtedly sought out the attractions of anonymous life in the big industrial towns, others of them continued by preference in the paths to which they were formerly constrained, as carpenters or ropeworkers. They may have overheard a ribald, contemptuous song about their alleged failings. But the days of systematic persecution ended over the last century, and are now apparently gone — one hopes — forever.

The sufferings of the cagots seemed at one time likely to last forever. The origins of the condition, whatever it was, were lost in the night of pre-history; the superstitious terror roused by the victims was sunk deep into the largely illiterate peasantry; the church hierarchy seemed capable of dragging its feet forever; rational investigation was hampered by the mental corruption of the investigators. Yet in a relatively short period of the 19th century, without any notable scientific breakthrough, without any campaign of publicity, the disease and the terminology of the disease were suddenly obsolete.

Though it began as a popular superstition, the life of the cagot-fantasy was greatly extended by the verbal-play of learned ignorance. What was the trick chasse-goths=cagots but a game fantasy for the amusement of the semi learned? When one found in the Bible that Gehazi was cursed by the prophet through all his generations what was the easiest way to find those long-disappeared generations? Nothing easier: they must be the present scum of the earth somehow assembled in southwestern France after a couple of thousand years. The inherent logic of persecution is short range. Effect can be cited as cause when they stand cheek by jowl. Cagots must smell bad because they are segregated in church. Cagots must be infectious because they wear badges and are forced to live in asylums. In the material world cause normally precedes effect, and it is hard to see that in the world of the mind effect so often precedes cause and invents the hypothetical, shadowy cause it is unable to perceive. Besides, in the folklore of disease several different conditions can easily be bundled together in a single packet and cured at a stroke. For centuries, the generic term "scrofula" served to describe tuberculosis of the joints and lymph glands but was used as well for secondary symptoms like inflammation of the skin and in the generic sense of "morally corrupt." For a long time it was known from a supposed magic cure, as "the king's evil;"' as late as 1712. Young Samuel Johnson was touched for it (not at all successfully) by Queen Anne. Like the dreadful cagot-superstition, the fearful scrofula epidemic disappeared into thin air — or rather, splintered into a number of explicable and ultimately treatable ailments. The new science of immunology rendered hundreds of ailments obsolete in the 19th century, but it had no influence on the cagots, because they were not sick to start with. But why talk of the superstitions and follies of the past? Within my lifetime, American Blacks could not drink from a public water-fountain or be served at the counter of an American restaurant. Jews, supposed to diffuse an offensive odor were denied accommodation at hotels and membership in private club, while racially mixed athletes had to masquerade as Central Americans.

Persecutors of cagots had only the dimmest idea of infectious contamination, and used their vague half-knowledge to lead themselves ever further astray.

A popular current medical fantasy that puts to shame the old uproar over cagots focuses on second-hand tobacco smoke. Everyone knows what it is and has experienced it; nobody, literally nobody, can quantify it. People, even the most virtuous, do not live under laboratory conditions. How much second-hand tobacco smoke anyone breathes, in how diluted a form, over how long a period and with what mixture of other possible contaminants can hardly be estimated in even the crudest degree. There are people who say they cannot endure to be even briefly in the presence of someone who hours ago passed a few minutes in the presence of a third party who had smoked a part of a cigarette. Who measures the many other different threats that we absorb over a lifetime from the atmosphere, the water, the mere presence of other human beings? Who assigns, and on what evidence, a particular malignant effect to a particular originating cause? Who compares statistically the differing effects of anxiety over contamination with the various consequences of contamination itself?

Anxiety ailments are well known to doctors and, though they are often pooh-poohed by the insensitive healthy, are not necessarily as bad for the patient as bothersome to his intimates and acquaintances. Along the lines of old wives' wisdom, the best recipe for longevity is often a reliable chronic complaint. There's nothing like it to keep the mind concentrated and occupied. The cagots were a fine scapegoat for 16th-century worriers — not as helpless or picturesque as witches, but just as serviceable. In our own age we have cause enough for anxiety in the great incurable epidemic that is blotting out our species, a continent at a time, not in fantasy but in countable corpses. With such overwhelming, tangible menaces to hand, the little anxieties and distractions of our civilized existence need be no more substantial than a curl of smoke. Peering through the haze of present worry, I seem to see nothing uglier than some blotches of polluted land set aside here and there on the green earth for warehousing incurables, pariahs, untouchables, and the miscellaneous unclean.

◆

# VI  HOMAGE TO CYRENE

he city of Cyrene in North Africa, in the region currently known as Libya, has to be located in time as well as space. It no longer exists as a city, and has not done so for a millennium and a half. I myself have never visited it, or even come close to doing so; yet it has lived in my imagination for better than half a century — whether in spite of, or because of, the fact that it has for me almost no material existence at all.

Using familiar coordinates, the site lies in eastern Libya on the Marmarica Peninsula, about ten miles from the Mediterranean Sea, between Bengazi and Tobruk. That, at least, is where it used to be, between roughly 650 B.C. and 400 A.D. Though there is a great deal of mythical and problematic material about the early story of Cyrene, the city seems to have been founded by some wandering Pelasgians, a name very loosely used by the early Greeks for bands of prehistoric settlers and drifters who infested the seas and raided the territories of the early Greek settlers. After the Trojan war, so the story runs, a group of these Pelasgi tried to settle near Sparta, to which they said they could trace their ancestry. The Spartans were by no means open-handed in their welcome of the strangers, and talked rather plainly of attacking the intruders with sword and spear; but the diplomatic Pelasgi offered to consult the oracle of Apollo at Delphi, which advised them that they must found a city of their own in Libya. This was a stunner, since most of the Pelasgi had no notion where Libya was. But the oracle reinforced its directive by imposing a long-continuing drought on the place where the Pelasgi were camping. The leader of the exile band, named Grinus, expostulated with the oracle, saying that he was too old to lead any such expedition; let one of the younger men be in charge, he said, and in making his argument he was understood to gesticulate at a young fellow named Aristoteles, who was not properly on the delegation at all, but had come along to seek from the oracle assistance in correcting a bad stutter. No matter: at the instigation of the oracle, the young man was renamed "Battus," which in the Libyan dialect was understood to mean "king." In due course the new king did in fact lead across the Mediterranean several boatloads of ex-Pelasgi, and not only became their king but founded a dynasty which endured, with interesting modifications, for several hundred years.

At first the wanderers tried to settle on an island named Platea, which they thought would satisfy the directives of the oracle by providing a place to build a city in Libya. Not so, however. The drought persisted on their new island, and on reapplying to the oracle, they were told they had not gone far enough into the mainland. With the aid of some friendly natives they actually marched about ten miles inland to a big spring called "The Fountain of Apollo." The oracle had told them, in what seemed random words, that they must settle "between water and water," and this requirement they thought they had met by settling on an island; but to fix their new home between the desert spring and the ocean shore appeared to work much better. So there, on what is known nowadays as the Jebl Akhdar, they put down their roots after what might have seemed a helter-skelter journey, but which gave destiny plenty of chance to assert itself. They named their new home Cyrene after a wood-nymph with interesting backgrounds. (She was of Thessalian origin but had been patronized by Apollo, which raised her above provincial distinctions.)

The new home of the settlers was not only far enough from the sea to provide seclusion from pirates and marauders, it was perched atop a 1,500-foot cliff which rose abruptly on the ocean side but then sloped gradually inland toward the desert. The land was well enough watered to support a scattering of forests, grains, and vines, as well as a completely unexpected bonus in the form of the wild herb silphium. It is (or was, for it is long extinct) delicious to eat and therapeutic for a wide range of conditions. Though it became extinct even before the city of Cyrene itself, silphium in the early days of the colony was like a blessing and a promise; on a more worldly level, it was also an important article of commerce. The Cyrenians built two useful and defensible harbor-towns within reach of their main city; they built not only subterranean walls and impressive tanks for storage of the region's scant rainfall; they raised also elegant temples to their gods and cultivated with particular success the very Greek art of sculpture. Perhaps because the great Pharaonic library of Alexandria was within relatively easy reach, literature flourished in Cyrene beyond what might have been expected of such a frontier outpost. The city was remote from most of its cultural roots. Only a few miles to the south, the plateau on which Cyrene was built tailed off into shifting sands over which restless Berbers ranged, but where nobody else could survive. From the east Cyrene was subject to attack by the Egyptians any time a Pharaoh or a Ptolemy felt ambitious, or was himself under pressure from further east. Participation in the Mediterranean trade contributed to the city's prosperity, but led to frequent conflict with commercial rivals both near at hand (Alexandria) and farther away (Carthage). Cyrene's own visible success led to the establishment in Northeast Libya of commercial rivals, a cluster of five cities known as the Pentapolis, none of them overwhelmingly powerful individually, but collectively strong enough to erode, over time, the central city's preeminence. Mostly the new towns were built along the seacoast, where they effectively shortstopped much of the trade that used to flow in and out of Cyrene. This was an aspect of the new location that apparently had not occurred to the oracle.

Trails leading into the interior or along the seashore were thin and scanty; travelers had to depend on widely spaced oases which might dry up without warning. The harbors that Cyrene constructed for her own use were supplanted by lesser centers, smaller but more numerous. Marginal rainfall and distant markets cut down on Cyrene's output; the precious silphium died out. Arrangements with the native Libyans, after an earlier period of relative harmony, deteriorated. For a while, it seems, Greeks and Libyans had alternated in the kingship of the community under the national titles of Battus and Arcesilaus. But the arrangement was too simple and perhaps too sensible to last, and the Cyrenians inevitably added civil war to their other accumulating misfortunes. Finally, the brutal ending of the Jewish War of Independence (formalized by the destruction of the Temple in 70 A.D.) brought terrible suffering to Jewish communities in Egypt, Cyprus, and Cyrene which had lent their support to the losing cause. The Jews of Cyrene are not much mentioned before the hour of their destruction, but they were clearly an important part of this small, highly commercialized settlement, and their crushing left the town little more than a rubble-covered waste land.

Under the advancing sands of the Sahara, Cyrene reverted to the barren desert it had originally been. Arab, Persian, and Egyptian conquerors rolled over the ruins of Cyrene, often without pausing to realize that it had once been a city. By the end of the fourth century A.D., the eloquent Synesius, a native of Cyrene who prided himself on his descent from the Spartan kings, described the city as one vast ruin, picked over by nomadic Arabs in search of discarded knick-knacks. What can be known, after 1,500 years, of a city battered so long ago into virtual nonexistence? The big outlines are long gone, beyond even the possibility of reconstruction; at best a few of the qualities of individual achievements can be glimpsed through the mists of time; at most an image of the city's character can be assembled.

At its height of prosperity, Cyrene was a city of some 100,000 citizens. Its basic character was Greek but much diluted from the beginning. It had little countryside to draw upon and was therefore decisively urban; its politics were influenced by its Spartan origins, but gradually, as commercial interests predominated, leaned more and more toward oligarchy. Strong though its trading interests were, Cyrene never had a sufficient base to support a metropolitan population, or to dominate the important north-south and east-west trade routes which crossed so near its walls and ports. What Cyrene could cultivate were the minor arts, the lesser articles of trade, luxuries — spices, dates, gum, feathers, silks, manuscripts, nuances, abstract ideas, a tradition of manners. Perhaps, in addition to time, distance, and historical destruction, which render all things hazy, the outline of Cyrene is blurred by its own deliberate delicacy of touch.

Cyrenians were no more capable of forming themselves into a "school" than of making themselves into an empire. The three best known of their writers could not possibly have known one another or influenced each other's thinking more than marginally. Still, Aristippus the philosopher who studied with Socrates developed (as we learn from his pupils) a nuanced and delicate form of hedonism; and this was by no means alien to the feelings cultivated by Callimachus, the poet who insisted his muse must remain trim and slender; while Synesius, who lived much later and was actually a Christian, wrote the most civilized of his apologies for a religion which hardly as yet deserved it. These three men had little or nothing in common, yet if, by some freak of time, they could have been assembled at a single symposium, one cannot doubt that they would have made a thoroughly congenial drinking party. Perhaps this is only a fleeting fancy, but there is about these three writers a delicate verbal touch, a quiet lack of self-assertion, that could have made them good friends.

## I. ARISTIPPUS

Though he was in some respects the most influential and discussed of the three Cyrenians, Aristippus the hedonist philosopher is least known through his writings, for the simple reason that none of them survive.[1]

He wrote a great many treatises and their titles are recorded; but of his texts, absolutely nothing. He lived early (from roughly 435 to 346 A.D.), which puts him at nearly a thousand years from the biographical compendium of Diogenes Laertius, who is our chief surviving authority for the lives of the ancient philosophers. Aristippus also lived most of his life, and all the latter part of it, in out-of-the-way Cyrene, where there was no such rich compost of gossip and anecdote as provided Diogenes with most of his biographical materials. In fact, the "Life of Aristippus is notably scanty. It provides no date for Aristippus' birth and no mention of his parents. Everybody with a Greek name in Cyrene must have mitigated there from some part of the mainland Greece; we no nothing of Aristippus' ancestry. The ancient biography provides no dates and only the vaguest indication of periods in Aristippus' life. We are told that he spent some time at the court of Dionysus, the tyrant of Syracuse; so did Plato, but we have no indication of when or why Aristippus left. Diogenes Laertius attributes twenty-odd books to the pen of Aristippus I, but he cites none of them, though he does quote from titles not included in the list, such as *The Luxury of the Ancients* (!V, 69) and *On the Physicians* (VIII, 21). Both are said to be diatribes against the predecessors of Aristippus, though from other sources we learn that Aristippus was noted for the courtesy of his manners. Several of the repartees and snappy sayings that Diogenes Laertius attributes to Aris-

---

1) This absolute blank with regard to the writings of a much-admired exponent of hedonism suggests the sinister hand of censorship. Perhaps an enthusiast for the priority of Epicurus was responsible; perhaps an exponent of the conventional morality. For sure, it's extraordinary that nothing at all survives of Aristippus' writings.

tippus are assigned in other parts of his book to other philosophers. Again, Diogenes Laertious says that Aristippus frequented prostitutes and answered sharply those who rebuked him for doing so; yet, at the same time (Diogenes says) he raised his daughter Areté to the highest standards of moral delicacy. How these stories fit together is not clear: a practicing whoremaster who preaches moral delicacy can hardly be supposed to teach anything but hypocrisy. Diogenes' "Life" of Aristippus is by no means long, and a good deal of it is devoted to describing the lives and works of his disciples. Yet the account tells us very little of these disciples — we are left to guess whether they congregated at Cyrene to sit about the famous philosophical garden, or corresponded with the master from different districts of the Mediterranean. Aristippus himself, it appears, suffered some opprobrium because he took money for his teachings — was, in other words, one of the first of the sophists, But there is reason to think that his charges, like the fees imposed by modern psychiatrists, were part of the therapy; they served to make his students think long and hard about the value of their studies.

Though the biographer barely mentions the fact, the career of Aristippus divides sharply in at least three parts. He was in Athens when very young as a disciple of Socrates, till the death of the latter (399 B.C., when Aristippus was more or less 26); then he was at the court of Dionysus in Syracuse, he was with the courtesan Lais at Corinth, he was with the satrap Artaphenes in Asia for an undetermined period. He returned to Cyrene some time around 390 or 380 B.C., and lived there with his wife and children till his death in 346. The advantage of this approximate, and in some measure suppositious, time frame is that it enables us to place the stories about Aristippus, particularly the one-liners and witty sayings, at different periods of the philosopher's life. Jumbled together, as Diogenes Laertious had them, they make impossible a coherent view of his character and of his life. But this is work for each interested investigator to perform on his own.

To be the father of *Areté* (Virtue) may have seemed significant to Aristippus because as a philosopher he was an undeviating exponent of *hédone* or pleasure. Pleasure, he said, was a first principle of human life, to be pursued constantly and with one's fullest intelligence. Any man who openly professes such a philosophy is bound to be caricatured as a bestial swine, a gross voluptuary, a grovelling beast. These are the mildest epithets that were attached to Epicurus, the later contemporary of Aristippus, and horrifying "eye-witness" accounts were often applied to that high-minded, meticulous philosopher. That no such vilification was ever attached to Aristippus is an important fact — negative, to be sure, but nonetheless indicative. He advocated, it would seem, pleasure but not debauchery, keen appreciation of the senses but not gluttony, quality not quantity.

There are various formulas by which hedonists may separate themselves from the unthinking, self-indulgence that comes naturally to most of mankind. None of these formulas are very complex, and Aristippus, so far as we can judge from his students, used most of them. Some pleasures involve consequences so disagreeable that, on balance, they cease to be pleasures at all. Within the philosophical mind itself there exists, or can be cultivated, a principle of moderation or prudence that enables us to qualify our own excessive desires. It draws reinforcement from the conventions and inhibitions of society — not from Mrs. Grundy, necessarily, but from people whom one respects and admires outside the immediate occasion. Aristippus was respected in his days as an ascetic voluptuary (so to speak) — one who cultivated the nuances of pleasure, the fines edges of self-indulgence. There have been voluptuaries whose pursuit of the exquisite drop of pleasure has been carried to the point of self-torture. Such was *not* Aristippus — no Des Esseintes before his time — but his advocacy of pleasure did embrace a principle of self-criticism and in the end of negation. It embraced as well — it must have — a principle of variation and novelty. Nothing is more boring and insipid than the same pleasure many times repeated. It is not just the moralists who make this point, but the voluptuaries themselves, the great seducers and debauchers, the dedicated gourmands. The pleasure they cultivate single-mindedly turns to ashes, their senses are overloaded, incitements to ecstasy turn to provocations of disgust. One of the most fatal objections to a philosophy of pleasure is the necessity of constant novelty.

Aristippus may not himself have completed the full cycle of discovery — novelty-excess-satiety-disgust-withdrawal — but the full pattern of his life is compatible with it. His long last residence at Cyrene, between the edge of the desert and the margin of the sea, must have meant something. A true addict of sensual pleasure would have taken a garden apartment on a fashionable boulevard within easy reach of delicatessens, pastry cooks, seafood shops, greengrocers and fruiterers, not to mention dancing girls, dubious boys, and other purveyors of sexual delicacies. To worship pleasure in Cyrene is to limit oneself automatically to the delights of a small town. Aristippus took no notice of gaudy performance, luxurious garments, or grandiose displays. Of the stupefying drugs he was, for better or worse, altogether innocent.

Because it emphasizes the physical pleasures which are accessible to everyone, hedonism has a perceptible affinity with skepticism. The pleasures of life which are available without prolonged meditation naturally look even better when one has concluded that meditation is in the nature of things futile. In any event, the gently skeptical element in Aristippus was transmitted to another Cyrenian, Carneades, and from him made its way to Cicero. This is a tangible genealogy, though it is not documented by a great deal of paper.

At best, philosophy is ill at ease in dealing with pleasure. When it urges us to indulge, it endorses the pressures of nature which in different individuals differently circumstanced are differently and unknowably forceful. Its voice is inevitably schoolmarmish because filtered through a generalizing vocabulary even when not deliberately pedagogic. In the matter of indulgence or abstinence, there is no better guide than experience or temperament, the knowledge an individual has of himself or acquires precisely by indulging or abstaining. As often as not, general rules guide one astray, or at least in unforeseeable directions. In the affairs of this world, we are solicited daily by an infinitude of pleasures whose gratifications and disadvantages we have to measure for ourselves on a sliding scale at whose readings we can only guess.

Perhaps, then, we do not lack so very much if we do not have even one of the twenty-three volumes that Aristippus is said to have penned. He is known to have advocated a life of pleasure; we can guess at the sort of pleasure he had in mind — sensual pleasure with a little qualification of elegance and good taste. These predilections were not in the formal sense philosophical; they were more in the line of being popular directives toward a possible life style. Problems of being, of cosmology, of politics, of ethics and morality Aristippus did not, so far as we can discover, meditate. If he thought about pleasure, it was not to any profound or systematic effect. Perhaps he liked to think about pleasure because it was too various and mutable and evanescent to allow him to reach any formal conclusions. He did not set much of an example for systematic thinkers. But he did set a sort of example for those who assume philosophy is to be lived as well as thought, that it is mutable and intimate so long as it is alive. Like Montaigne, Aristippus was only marginally a philosopher, but mostly an experimenter in modes of the good life. It is only a guess, but he might not have minded greatly the demise of his written books because he thought of them all (perhaps) as informal essays. He should have had a chance to try the title out.

## II. CALLIMACHUS

Callimachus was a native of Cyrene, a descendant by his own account of the royal family of the first king, Battus; yet almost the first thing we learn of him is that he deserted his native town and moved to Alexandria. Some say because his first employment at Alexandria was as a school teacher, he must have arrived in the capital in a state of penury. But there are two sides to that coin,' perhaps Cyrene itself had reached such depths of degradation and squalor that the descendant of her first king felt humiliated at the thought of remaining there. In any event, Callimachus did not arrive in Alexandria as the proverbial *Graeculus esuriens* (hungry Greeklet). He had his own school, not of urchins, but of aspiring litterateurs; he was popular and respected, and soon became the center of an admiring circle. As a result, the ruling Ptolemy, surnamed Philadelphus, appointed him to a post in the great Alexandrian library. Probably he was not its head but he held a respectable and sufficiently paid position. His task was to catalogue chronologically the manuscripts in that vast collection, and catalogue he did, producing over the years of his service fully 120 volumes of listings. He had helpers, no doubt, but it was an immense and valuable task. At the same time he wrote poetry in a great variety of meters and forms, while continuing to advise those who came to him for literary advice. His life and writings were bound up with the court of Alexandria, which centered in turn on the urbane but far from vigorous Ptolemy and his much-admired queen Arsinoe. It was a civilized and cosmopolitan society of officials and courtiers who gathered around the throne of Ptolemy. For this audience Callimachus wrote ceremonial and official poems, as well as poems of frequently obsequious compliment (not unlike those expected of any laureate), as well as poems expressing his own responses to the occasions of his life. A few hymns survive, a goodly number of epigrams, a book about *Origins* which survives in fragments, and an equally fragmented romantic epic, *Hecale* — a very substantial body of poetic work, if we had more than a small fraction of it.

For though Callimachus enjoyed during his lifetime as much admiration as was good for him, time was not kind in the years after his death. His epigrams were scattered and neglected, many of them buried in mountains of what was obviously considered waste paper. Tax records, property deeds, and similar inert material obscured, but over the years preserved, bits of the words of Callimachus, along with even more precious fragments by poets such as Sappho. This material was first recognized as significant in the latter part of the 19th century — with the result that much of Callimachus' work, though more than two thousand years old (by the calendar), has been made publicly accessible only within the last century.

It should be added that Callimachus was not exempt from criticism even during his lifetime. His quarrel with Apollodorus, originally his pupil, raised big waves in the small fishpond of ancient literary opinion. It involved nothing more subtle than a question of literary dimensions. Apollodorus had in mind to write, and ultimately did write, a poem on the epic scale. It was not Homeric, but its four books and spacious themes did qualify it as an epic, by intent at least. Callimachus was provoked, probably less by the venture itself than by incautious words that Apollodorus spoke in defense of his own proceedings. The testy response of Callimachus is preserved: he said, in effect, "a big book is a big pile of ——." Not surprisingly, the younger man took offense and sailed off in dudgeon to the island from which he ultimately took his surname, Apollonius Rhodius.

Meanwhile Callimachus remained in Alexandria cataloguing his books and writing the erudite, allusive little poems that were his personal delight. It is quite possible to think that Apollonius got the better of the argument (his *Argonautica* was well received, and continued for many years to be admired and imitated), but Callimachus retained his intimate audience of effete Alexandrian erudites. Whether this sort of audience was a good or bad thing for his poetry remains moot. Many verdicts on his poetry run to the effect that it is learned, laborious, and leaden. But there are exceptions to this judgement, and questions about the people who propound it. It is by no means certain that Callimachus was inhibited, any more than Mallarmé, by the over-cultivated, super-subtle audience for which he wrote. In any event, not everybody can write in the heroic vein who wants to. The Alexandrians cultivated small forms, not just in the instance of Callimachus but for general reasons extremely difficult to define. The idylls of Theocritus and the prose romances that descend from Milesian tales evidently appealed to the

taste of Alexandrian times. If we think of Alexandrian taste as developing gradually and variously, not by any single decision, neither
Callimachus not the alexandrines will seem to need very much explaining.

One major poem by Callimachus seems designed to compromise, if
not bridge, the gap between long and short poems. It is the collection
titled *Aetia* or *Origins*, and it survives for the most part in fragments,
some as small as a single line or a mere half-line of verse. The biggest
pieces are a scant hundred lines. Enormous effort and ingenuity has
gone into assembling and relating these fragments; many suggested
connections still remain elusive. It seems clear that the total poem on
origins amounted to some 7,000 lines in four books, each consisting of a
different number of variously sized units (*aetia*). The sorts of things
investigated are mainly curious customs of different people or districts,
myths which explain rituals, odd words or phrases, and popular usages
or superstitions. Sometimes Callimachus speaks in his own person,
describing voyages he has made to look into some subject; often he
assumes the character of an imaginary person or even the imagined
voice of a property of the story. Woven into these narratives are many
allusions to the history and mythology of Cyrene, the poet's native city.
Some of the poems were clearly mock-heroic in tonality, as a detailed
account of making an elaborate mouse-trap; others are elevated in tone,
as befits a narrative about the gods and their doings. All the *aetia* are in
elegiac meter. The best known is the last, the so-called "Coma Berenices"
or "Lock of Berenice," the title being an afterthought, and the poem itself
being best known from an imitation/translation of it by Catullus (#66).
About seventeen lines out of an estimated hundred or so remain of the
original Greek.

In other words, the poem survives as a fragment of which we
possess only a smaller fragment. There is no knowing if Callimachus'
poem as he wrote it began as abruptly as in both the Greek and Latin it
now does. It appears to be a high-pitched lament by the tress cut from
Berenice's head. The story behind this visionary scene, to which the
poem makes frequent allusion, is as follows. Berenice was a daughter of
King Magas of Cyrene, married to Ptolemy Euergetes. On his departure
to lead his troops in the third Syrian War (247-246 B.C.), she vowed to
dedicate a lock of her hair for his safe return; in the interim she placed
it in the temple of Arsinoe Aphrodite at Zephyrium near Lake Canopus.
Someone stole the lock, or at any rate it disappeared; Conon the astrono-

mer was consulted, perhaps on the score that he was reputed a wise man and after some meditation he located it high in the heavens within the space defined by Ursa Major, Bootes, Virgo, and Leo. The constellation is a tiny but distinct grouping of stars; to have discovered it without the help of any optical devices gives one special respect for the powers of Conon.

Most of what ones says about the poem of Callimachus has to be tentative, since it depends largely on the version of Catullus, whose accuracy in following the subtleties of a poem two hundred years old is not to be taken for granted. It is known, for instance, that the last few lines, describing the orgiastic welcome home of the triumphant troops to Alexandria, were not in the original. Whether Catullus had any warrant for inventing them, apart from his own poetic feeling about what Callimachus was up to, cannot be told for sure.

Still, Catullus was not the man to be drawn to a leaden piece of obsolete courtly compliment, if that were all Callimachus' poem had been. In fact, the speech making up the poem as a whole is a wild and passionate lament, displaced by the vehement art of Callimachus from Berenice herself to the lock of her hair, and raised from the earth to the highest heavens, raised also in poetic terms to the height of language's expressive power. The whole atmosphere of the sudden opening is at once barbaric and imaginatively abstract, like Mallarmé's "Cantique de Saint Jean." It is not unusual in Greek poetry for an object set up to commemorate someone to speak (in the poem) and celebrate the departed by explaining itself. But this is not the scheme of Callimachus' poem. The tress does not represent a deceased person, and it is not placed conveniently by the side of the road for passersby to read. It does not mediate or exemplify; it wants to get back down to earth.

Schematically viewed (as it seems to demand), the "Coma Berenices" begins high in the inaccessible heavens and ends with the tress wishing to be, and finally actually being, ecstatically reunited with her mistress on earth. Thus it could be argued that the concluding lines added by Catullus without authorial warrant actually fulfill the movement of the poem. From earth to heaven and back again, the poem completes its orbit. It belongs in a collection titled "Origins" because it explains a lofty celestial phenomenon by the facts of Cyrene's turbulent dynastic history — a history with which Conon at least may not have been all that familiar. As for the poem itself, it remains a delicate and glittering image, despite the many obstacles across which one must strive to reach it. Indeed, it exemplifies some favorite injunctions of Apollo, which Callimachus loved to repeat — to "keep the Muse slender," and to "avoid the beaten tracks of others" by "singing among those who love the brilliance of the cicada, not the raucous noise of asses."

### III. SYNESIUS

By the time Synesius was born in Cyrene (approximately 370 A.D.) there cannot have been much left of the original city. Like Callimachus, Synesius claimed descent from the Spartan founders, but made no attempt to assert political authority, if indeed there was any left to assert. As a scholar and thinker he naturally gravitated toward Alexandria, where he entered he neo-Platonic academy and came under the influence of the celebrated Hypatia. She was the daughter of the astronomer Theon, and in her own right a teacher of distinction. In the end, she fell victim to the ugliest form of *odium theologicum*, being dragged from her chariot while passing through the streets of Alexandria and hideously assassinated by a screaming mob of Christians inflamed by St. Cyril. Her sin had been friendship with Orestes, the pagan prefect of the city. Synesius, who had some years earlier been named bishop of Ptolemais, was lucky enough to die of natural causes the year before he could have seen his co-religionists at their horrible worst.

He was, it would seem, a provincial patrician, born to wealthy parents, given the best possible education, and viewed from early manhood as a person of exceptional promise. Barely had he completed his schooling at Alexandria when he was dispatched (397) on a mission to represent the Pentapolis at the court of the emperor Arcadius at Constantinople. Technically his mission involved tax grievances and trade policies, and the complications were insistent enough to extend his stay in Constantinople to three years. He took advantage of this leisure to compose and deliver to emperor Arcadius an oration containing, in addition to general advice on the dangerous times, some gentle thoughts on the wisdom of tolerating Christianity. Synesius was by no means at this stage a fully converted Christian but he saw, as not everybody did, the advantages of bringing together peaceloving people in defense of peace. After Synesius' mission to Constantinople was successfully completed, he returned to North Africa, but deliberately settled neither in Cyrene nor in Alexandria, rather on an isolated family estate well out of both towns, where he could cultivate his personal library and exercise himself at the chase. In 403 he married. Marriage was not an absolute impediment to a position in the Christian church, but it was a difficulty to be negotiated away when the proposal came up, in 410, to appoint him bishop of Ptolemais.

In fact both his diversions were more strenuous than in his account of them they appeared. While hunting the local gazelles he had to remain alert against occasional warlike tribesmen in small but desperate encounters. And in the quiet of his library he had to work out the quality of his commitment to points of Christian doctrine toward which his neo-Platonism inclined him but could not commit him. When offered the bishopric at Ptolemais, he began by firmly stipulating that he would not under any circumstances put away his wife. There were, as always legalistic and ecclesiastical arguments, but Synesius took as the cornerstone of his position the fact that he was fond of her. Then he insisted on retaining some highly technical and not wholly orthodox views on speculative matters like the creation of the soul, the final destination of the material world, and the resurrection of the body. These matters he agreed not to discuss publicly, lest they unsettle the faithful; but he insisted on holding his own opinions privately, as a philosopher. Evidently, the church had more need of Synesius than he did of the church; but after much argument, the trends of which can be followed in the private letters which survive, ultimately he accepted the office and was duly confirmed.

The position of a bishop was no sinecure in the Pentapolis, any more than elsewhere in those early days. Synesius had to defend his flock against the same unpredictable raiders as had disturbed his hunting expeditions, and he had also to defend against the secular (Roman) government his right to offer asylum to fugitives. His life was darkened by the loss of his wife; and the kind of sectarian fury that would later destroy Hypatia cannot have been absent from the last years of Synesius' life. Yet he fought to survive, and not only to survive but to maintain his civilized good humor. As a jape he wrote a mildly funny, mock-formal elocution in praise of baldness. It was his own condition, and of little importance in itself; yet it brings us (strangely) closer to his gentle, humorous temper than any number of weightier treatises could have done.

Gibbon makes rather ponderous fun of Synesius' allocution before the emperor Arcadius as absurdly idealistic and impractical. That is one point of view, though it is asking a lot of a young man, barely thirty, to address the ruler of half the world in words of ripe political wisdom. Sysnesius was, for a fact, a young man unhardened in the ways of the brutal world. Yet if Arcadius had been half the man his father Theodosius was, the advice he got from Synesius could have been salutary indeed.

Synesius lived at a period of history and in a corner of the world where the luminaries of intellect did not penetrate. He was by no means what modern political wiseacres would call a "wimp;" but he does not create the impression of a solid, impressive figure. He did not build for himself an identity. At the end of his essay on Dio the sophist, Synesius admits half-ashamedly to a habit of thought, unusual enough in antiquity, but which rather endears him to a modern reader:

> Oft times I do not attempt to await the conclusion of a book for any good it may do me, but rather do I lift up my eyes and proceed to exercise myself in the narrative, not hesitating in the least but yielding to the opportune moment; and pretending that I am reading straight on, I recite out of my own head whatever it seems to me should follow, and I test what has thus been said in the light of what has been written. Oft times I find that I have happened upon the same sense and even the same form of expression (as the author). On the other hand, I have occasionally made a happy shot at a thought, though missing the phrasing itself, and have produced what quite resembled the harmony of the work.

The divertimenti of Synesius would be interesting to have; he had exactly the spirit of the form.


IV   THE STATUE

The "Venus of Cyrene" — so called — was discovered in 1913 amid the ruins of the ancient Thermae, and (Libya being at the time under Italian domination) made her way inevitably to the Museo delle Terme in Rome. There is not very much literature about her, in the form of fact or fancy. Her making can be dated only approximately to the Hellenistic age, though she may (alternately) be a copy of Roman provenance. No doubt her maker was trained in the traditions of classical Greek sculpture, but there is no definitively Greek sculpture that is quite like the Lady of Cyrene. The name of the sculptor is beyond even the reach of conjecture. She may well represent Venus rising from the waves (Anadyomene), and that is the name by which she had gone since her disinterment. But against this identification stand her location in the public baths, the Thermae, and the substantial support, in the form of a dolphin posing on its nose, over which she drapes her vestments. This does not make the best of sense if she is rising from the waves, newborn. On the other hand, she may not be an Olympian at all, but a material woman, drying her hair or preparing to dry it, after immersion in the caldarium. She is a magnificent female, not quite of Maillol proportions, and very much free-standing. The dolphin by her side may remind us tangibly that Aphrodite rose from the sea, or it may equally remind us that Cyrene was the daughter of the river Peneus in Thessaly, and in Libya the beloved of Apollo whose spring gave life to the desert soil (between water and water) on which the city of Cyrene was founded. It has always seemed to me that the slightly flat-footed posture assumed by the statue identifies the figure more with the mortal, stable earth than with the restless salt sea. Truth to tell, there is no way to say positively which mythological figure our piece of stone unequivocally represents. But I like her as Cyrene because in that aspect she is more equivocal. Cyrene was in fact the mother, by Apollo, of Aristeias, to whom we are indebted for such useful arts as healing, prophecy, rain-making, and bee-keeping. This utilitarian lady is a proper emblem of the city for which, as far as the legends go, Venus never had a kind thought. It is pleasant to think of this warm nymph presiding over, while buried beneath, a town all too mortal, but with its own silver vitality during its allotted span.

To call our statue the "Cyrene" of Cyrene would not be half bad.

◆